"Close the door. I want to talk to you."

Obediently, Serena did as she was told, looking up at Nick hotly through her lashes.

He walked toward her, and said deeply, "I don't have much time. I want to sign this deal and get the wheels moving on it. But there's an essential ingredient in the package that I don't yet have."

"I don't understand," she said huskily.

"Yes, you do," he said thickly, watching her.

Nick suddenly lifted his strong hands to her face, making her gasp, staring up at him as he said under his breath, "You're the essential ingredient, Lady Serena. You. That's why I've asked you here now. I'm prepared to invest millions in Flaxton Manor—but only on one condition." His blue eyes slipped to her mouth as he said, "That you agree to be my wife."

red pyjama trousers and bare chest. 'Morning,' he said

SARAH HOLLAND was born in Kent and brought up in London, England. She began writing at eighteen because she loved the warmth and excitement of Harlequin. She has traveled the world, living in Hong Kong, the south of France and Holland. She attended a drama school, and was a nightclub singer and a songwriter. She now lives on the Isle of Man. Her hobbies are acting, singing, painting and psychology. She loves buying clothes, noisy dinner parties and being busy.

SARAH HOLLAND

Ruthless Lover

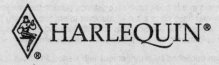

HARLEQUIN®

TORONTO • NEW YORK • LONDON
AMSTERDAM • PARIS • SYDNEY • HAMBURG
STOCKHOLM • ATHENS • TOKYO • MILAN • MADRID
PRAGUE • WARSAW • BUDAPEST • AUCKLAND

Burke's Peerage

With thanks to Kate Lonsdale and Susan Goddard of *Burke's Peerage* for their considerable help regarding title, inheritance and protocol.

ISBN 0-373-18693-2

RUTHLESS LOVER

First North American Publication 1998.

Copyright © 1992 by Sarah Holland.

CHAPTER ONE

SERENA slid out of her black silk négligé and laid it carelessly on the antique chair. The long black lace nightgown skimmed her slender body with sensual elegance. In the mirrored wardrobe, she saw her long red-gold hair fall seductively over one eye and smiled ruefully. Her looks had always been at odds with her background.

Slipping into bed, she yawned. It had been a long day. Outside, New York was in the grip of a heat wave, and lit up like a cosmopolitan dream. The city that never sleeps, she thought with a faint smile, and switched off the light.

It was midnight, and she drifted into a warm reverie. The duvet was as cosy as a nest. Sleep claimed her and she began to dream, as she so often did, in bright colours, seeing oils on canvas and faces from her past turned into swirls of blue, gold, red...

When the bedroom door opened at three a.m. she did not stir. When the powerful male body got into bed beside her she gave a slight sigh, turning towards him.

But when the long hands slid over her waist and drew her gently against him she began to stir, her dream changing from paints and canvas to flesh, as a

figure in stark masculine colour came to life and began
making love to her.

Serena's red-gold head tilted back. A strong mouth
closed over hers, hard fingers slid over her throat, invoking shivers, and she moaned involuntarily as the
kiss forced her to respond, her slender body sliding
against his, feeling the sweet, hot rush of desire as she
encountered hard stomach, hair-roughened thighs, felt
his strong hands slide forcefully down to her slim hips.

Her breath came faster; she was moaning, drowning
in sensation as her hands moved up to his strong neck,
fingers pushing into thick hair, her body arching in
fierce arousal against his.

A rough sound of masculine desire echoed in the
dark bedroom; strong hands swept up over her breast,
and she gave a hoarse cry of excitement as she felt
that mouth, that real mouth close over hers with insis-
tent desire as his hands stroked her erect nipples.

Suddenly her brain flashed away from dreams and
into reality. Her lids flickered open to see the stark
silhouette of a man's face, the glitter of blue eyes terrifying her.

'No...!' Serena struggled, eyes stretched wide with
alarm, panic sending her into a frenzy as she kicked
and fought the aggressor in her bed then leapt away
with a hoarse cry, running for the door.

The bedside light was punched on by the intruder.

Serena turned, heart crashing at her breastbone, to
see Nick sitting up in bed, watching her with a lazy,
sardonic smile, his magnificent chest exposed by the
loose dark red robe he wore.

For a second, she just stared at him. His black hair

was tousled, his tough face filled with cynical mockery, his mouth a hard ruthless line.

'What are you doing here?' she demanded as rage flooded through her.

'Trying to sleep,' he drawled, running a hand through his black hair. 'What are you doing here?'

Her green eyes flashed at him. 'You're not supposed to be in New York! I was told you'd be in Washington this week!'

'There was a problem with the jet,' he said flatly. 'I was diverted to Kennedy. It was the middle of the night. What was I supposed to do—check into the Plaza?'

'You like the Plaza!' she said, struggling to get her chaotic emotions under control, horribly aware that she had responded like wildfire to his kiss and that he knew it.

He laughed sardonically. 'I love the Plaza. But I have a perfectly good apartment here, and I don't see why I shouldn't use it.'

'Because I'm here!' she said tightly, standing by the door, green eyes blazing at him. 'And you knew I was here! My schedule specified New York for the whole of this week.'

'So it did,' he said with soft mockery, and let his blue eyes slide with insolent sexual appraisal over her slender body. 'But I haven't seen you since Christmas, and I fancied a quick visit. Anything wrong with that?'

'You're not interested in seeing me,' she said angrily. 'You just came here to cause trouble! I don't know why, and I don't really care. But I won't be used to fill a boring night in your life, Nick, so you may as well just get dressed and call the Plaza!'

Turning, she walked out of the bedroom and into the living-room. She was shaking. Appalled, she stared down at her hands, normally so cool and competent, and saw the powerful tremor that was so uncontrollable.

How dared he do that? Imagine getting into bed with her and kissing her like that! He'd never done it before; never...

The door opened and she whirled, heart in her mouth.

'Don't give me orders, Serena,' Nick drawled, a threat of steel in his voice as he watched her, hands thrust in the pockets of his robe. 'I've always been the one in charge of this marriage, and that's not going to change now.'

Her mouth shook. 'You just broke the rules!' she accused hotly. 'You shouldn't have done that!'

'They're unwritten rules,' he said flatly. 'I can break them any time I like.'

Serena caught her breath at his arrogance. 'Oh, I see! Just because you've been prevented from meeting up with one of your mistresses for the night, you think you can come here and make your demands on me!' Her body trembled with inexplicable rage. 'Well, I won't have it!'

'It was only a kiss,' he drawled, steel-blue eyes mocking her.

'That's not the point!'

'A kiss you responded to very excitingly, Serena,'

he said softly, and the hot colour flooded up her neck to her face, leaving her breathless and unable to reply.

There was a brief, tense silence. Her pulses were racing disturbingly, and she felt for the first time that Nick had set their marriage on a different course—a course that terrified her.

After three years, he had suddenly taken the gloves off. She had always known, instinctively, that he might one day do it. But she had never expected it, not really, not in her deepest moments of contemplation.

This situation had all the hallmarks of disaster. She knew Nick was not going to defuse it. Therefore, she would have to be the one to take the necessary steps.

'Very well.' Serena lifted her red-gold head. 'If you refuse to do the decent thing by checking into the Plaza—I'll go instead.'

'Don't be ridiculous,' he said flatly. 'It's only for one night.'

'And where do you propose to sleep?' She arched red-gold brows.

'In one of the other bedrooms.' He shrugged broad shoulders, his manner indolent. 'We have four, after all.'

'Then why did you come to my room?' she asked under her breath, hating him. 'Why did you deliberately get into bed with me?'

He regarded her through heavy eyelids. 'I told you,' he said softly, 'I just fancied a kiss.'

Serena struggled to remain calm in the face of the potent sexual weapons he was turning on her. This situation was getting more dangerous by the second. She couldn't cope with it, and the look on his ruthless face told her that he knew it, and that he was doing it deliberately.

'Why are you doing this, Nick?' she asked under her breath, suddenly sensing the very real threat he had decided to unleash. 'It's deliberate, isn't it?'

He watched her, his face hard. 'Why should I deliberately jeopardise an arrangement that's worked so well for so long?'

Her gold lashes flickered. She felt suddenly uncertain. Yet Nick had kept his distance for three years. He had married her for her title, and then just walked away to his work, his mistresses and his busy life without a backward glance.

There had never been any pretence of mutual attraction between them. There had never been any tenderness, or love or hint of affection. For him to come here now and get into bed with her...

'You'll be leaving in the morning, then?' she asked unsteadily.

He inclined his dark head. 'First thing.'

Serena breathed a little more easily. 'Right...' She felt overwhelmingly conscious of her body in the revealing black silk nightdress, especially when Nick was looking at her like that, running his blue gaze with stark sexual appraisal over her. 'Then, if you don't mind, I think I'll move into the spare bedroom and—'

'There's no need for that,' he said coolly. 'I'll move.'

She expelled her breath on a sigh of silent relief. 'Thank you.'

Nick's hard mouth curved in a mocking little smile.

'No need to look as though you're going to faint with relief, darling!' he murmured, and strolled towards her.

Involuntarily she took a step backwards, staring at him in alarm.

Nick stopped, eyes narrowing. 'Are you afraid of me, Serena?'

Angrily, she lifted her red-gold head, meeting his cool blue gaze with a challenge. 'Why on earth should I be afraid of you?'

'Well, quite,' he said softly. 'We've been married for three years, and you've always treated me with cool indifference. So why the sudden look of alarm in your face?'

'Anger,' she corrected, arching her haughty brows. 'I'm angry with you for doing this.'

His gaze slid to the rise and fall of her breasts beneath the black silk low-cut neckline. Serena felt colour flood her face and her heart start thumping madly. It was so completely out of character for her to react to him like this that she started to shake again, staring at him, acutely aware of his powerful brand of masculinity for the first time.

'You show anger very excitingly, Serena,' he said under his breath, and raised his blue eyes to meet hers. 'I wonder what would happen if I—'

'Just go to bed, Nick!' she said hoarsely, stepping back from him, a quiver of powerful excitement in her full mouth.

He looked at her intently, his mouth a firm line, then nodded. 'Sure. It's three a.m. and we're both tired.'

Relief flooded her again. She gave a stiff nod. 'I

won't see you for breakfast, I take it? You'll be leaving on the first flight?'

'Of course,' he said coolly, and strode across the room towards the master bedroom, going in and closing the door behind him with a quiet click.

Serena stared at the closed door, her heart thumping. It was almost unbelievable that he had done this. To come here in the middle of the night and get into bed with her, start making love to her...

She felt so shaken that she knew going to sleep was impossible. In an effort to come to terms with what had just happened, she went to the kitchen, got a glass and poured herself a very small measure of brandy.

It stung the back of her throat. She enjoyed that sting, and the flood of warmth that came with it. It would help her relax a little, too, so she took it into her bedroom and got into bed, nursing it as she thought about what Nick had just done.

Three years ago, Serena had left a sheltered existence at an English country finishing school to find the shock of her life awaiting her. Her parents were so heavily in debt that Flaxton Manor and the entire estate would have to be sold.

Her parents, the Earl and Countess of Archallagen, were understandably in despair. The manor was a beautiful sixty-seven-room Tudor masterpiece, built in 1532 for a favourite of Anne Boleyn: Robert Flaxton, the Earl of Archallagen. Robert had been in love with Anne Boleyn, and her presence was everywhere, in the square courtyard with the statue of Anne, the minstrel's gallery and haunted chapel with her initials carved over the doors, and the Tudor rose laced through every oak-panelled room in the house. Robert Flaxton had managed to escape execution in 1536 by disappearing to France when Anne Boleyn was executed, and not returning until Henry VIII died. With his red hair and flashing green eyes, Robert had always had what was known as the Flaxton Luck.

When, over four hundred years later, the Manor fell to the edge of bankruptcy, Serena's parents' first thought was to open it to the public. But that would cost even more money. They would have to employ guides, build car parks, print guide-books, make extensive repairs—and the bank was already foreclosing on them.

'I know someone who might agree to bankroll you out of this,' the family accountant told them. 'An American multi-millionaire. Nick Colterne. He's rich, powerful and bored.'

'How can anyone be bored if they're rich and powerful?' Lord Archallagen commented drily.

'Because Nick Colterne is a living piece of dynamite! He reorganises companies for fun. Turns everything he touches to gold. He owns about seventy different corporations, and is always on the look-out for something new.'

'But would he be interested in saving a country estate in an English backwater?' her father sighed, running a gnarled hand over his eyes.

'I'll send him a fax,' the accountant promised. 'Outline the details, the financial angle, and see what he says.'

'Let's hope it's yes,' her father said grimly, 'or our home will be turned into a hotel or conference centre.'

Serena winced at the thought, her green eyes resting on her father with love. He was too old for this. At sixty, he was close to retirement age, and it showed in the weary droop of his shoulders, the silver eyebrows and old, gardening hands.

Her parents had had Serena late in life. 'Our little surprise,' they had always called her. She had been born when they were both in their forties, and her mother had had a traumatic confinement at the age of forty-two.

With her red-gold hair, slanting green eyes and full sensual mouth, Serena had been a surprise in more ways than one. Her mother was blonde, her father dark. The red hair was a throwback to Robert Flaxton, who had caught the heart and attention of Anne Boleyn for such a brief, golden moment.

Serena's looks were also distinctly at odds with her pedigree. As Lady Serena Flaxton, she was a 'surprise' to everyone who met her, because that flaming hair and the sensual curves of her slender body were completely unexpected in a young aristocrat.

Nick Colterne replied within twenty-four hours. He was interested, and would arrive to view the property in three days.

Flaxton Manor went into an uproar. The handful of old faithful staff still working there out of love for the Flaxton family were in a dither of excitement, dusting and polishing along with the rest of the family, desperate to save the estate from bankruptcy.

Nick Colterne arrived in a long black Cadillac limousine.

Serena watched from an upstairs window as he

stepped out, dark and dynamic with flashing blue eyes that ran over the Tudor walls with a look of narrowed interest.

Wow! she thought, feeling her heart quickening and her eyes flashing over him, seeing the hard-muscled shoulders, the ruthless mouth and the arrogant stride of his long muscular legs. Nick Colterne looked every inch a man; and fire flashed along her veins as her green eyes moved restlessly over him, wide and admiring.

Suddenly, he looked up and saw her. He stopped dead, staring at her. A powerful crackle of electricity ran through her, making her heart stop, breath cease…

She flushed to her hairline at the penetrating sexual insolence of his gaze as it flashed over her innocent young face, waist-length red hair falling across one eye.

Stepping back with a gasp, she slammed the window shut, trembling.

Downstairs, she heard him striding into the main hall, surrounded by henchmen, biting out instructions, sending them off to investigate while he spoke to her parents in the drawing-room.

He was obviously a whirlwind, Serena thought with a stab of excitement, and waited in her room to hear the outcome of the visit.

'I've never seen him so animated!' their accountant enthused that night. 'He's definitely interested.'

'Do you think he'll want to buy it from us, though?' her father said anxiously. 'We want to try and keep it in the family, you see.'

'That depends on whether it makes financial sense

to him,' the accountant said with a sigh. 'He'll take the biggest money-making option.'

'Even if it means we lose everything?' Serena asked passionately. 'Surely it would be kinder to loan us money and let us repay it over a period of years?'

The accountant laughed. 'Don't expect kindness from a man like Nick Colterne. He's a cynical cut-throat shark, swimming in the most dangerous financial waters of the world. He'll make you an offer of some sort—but whatever it is, you can be sure he'll be the one to benefit.'

Serena shuddered. 'He sounds ruthless...'

'He's not a charity, darling.' The Earl sighed, his face lined with strain. 'And we're not in a position to argue. We'll just have to take whatever he offers us.'

It was an appalling situation to be in, and Serena was frantic over the next twenty-four hours as they waited for Nick Colterne's decision.

He returned a day later with his Cadillac and his henchmen. In a black business suit he looked the epitome of the cynical business shark, a gold watch-chain glittering across his taut black waistcoat. He moved with all the arrogance of American money, his face tough, cynical and determined.

Serena watched him arrive, keeping herself carefully hidden. He glanced up at her bedroom window, and although she knew he could not possibly see her she felt his eyes narrow on her mouth, and a tremor went through her. Did he have X-ray vision?

The meeting with her parents went on and on. Serena waited in an agony of tension.

At six o'clock, Mottram, the maid, tapped on her

bedroom door. 'His lordship requests that you join him in the drawing-room,' she said primly, then gave a little cry of worry. 'Oh, Lady Serena! What's to become of us…?'

Serena tried to comfort the young girl, patting her shoulder. 'I don't know, Mottram. We can only pray…'

When she opened the drawing-room door, the first person she saw was Nick Colterne whirling to face her, his eyes racing over her body with that insolent sexual appraisal, and Serena felt breathless, closing the door shakily behind her.

'Ah! There you are, my dear!' Her father got up from one of the worn, patched armchairs and strolled towards her in his English tweeds. 'Mr Colterne wanted to meet you.'

He introduced Serena to Nick Colterne formally, and she stared at him through her gold lashes, pulses thudding as his powerful tanned hand closed over hers in a formidable grip.

'So what do I call you?' Nick drawled softly, blue eyes sliding to burn on her full mouth. 'Your ladyship?'

'That's rather complicated,' she replied huskily, unable to take her eyes off his powerful face and that hard, ruthless mouth.

'Oh, I love complications.' His cool Boston drawl was as dynamic as the rest of him. 'They make me want to sort them out, pronto.'

'British peerage is a minefield of protocol,' her father said with a vague smile. 'My daughter is an only child, and therefore will inherit my title.'

Her mother smiled. 'Not in a manner of speaking, darling. She'll inherit mine.'

'Of course, of course!' The earl rubbed his forehead. 'Serena will eventually become Countess of Archallagen.'

'Countess?' Nick's eyes widened.

'In her own right,' her father said with a vague smile.

'What about the man she marries?' Nick asked coolly.

'Well,' her father shrugged, 'he won't get a title, but any children my daughter has would certainly inherit it.'

Nick's blue eyes flicked back to Serena. He stepped a little closer. 'In the meantime—what do I call you?'

'Just Lady Serena,' she said softly, pulses leaping.

'That's very formal.' He flicked his insolent gaze to the full breasts which strained against the delicate silk dress she wore, and she felt her colour rise in fierce excitement at the way he dared look at her so boldly. 'What happens when we reach an informal footing?'

Serena blushed, lowering her lashes. 'That depends on how well you know me.'

'How well do I have to know you before I can call you Serena?'

'Very well indeed,' she said huskily.

He smiled, then reached out a strong hand and touched her hair. 'So, you're going to be a countess one day…' He trailed his long fingers through her hair, towering over her, eyes dark with blatant sexual desire. 'I've never met a red-headed countess before.'

Her parents stiffened, staring at him, and Serena

took an involuntary step back, green eyes stricken, sensing their disapproval of the way he touched her, and feeling guilty for having enjoyed it.

Nick's eyes narrowed, shooting quickly to her parents', and there was a brief, tense silence in the drawing-room as the legal papers remained unsigned on the Elizabethan carved table.

'Well,' Nick Colterne drawled, a hard smile curving his cynical mouth, 'it's been a long day, hasn't it? And I feel in need of a little recreation.' He glanced at the Rolex on his dark-haired wrist. 'I think I'd like to take your beautiful daughter out to dinner. Any objections?'

Her parents were very still, their faces grim as they looked at Serena, standing before him like a sacrifice.

Serena went to dinner with him, deeply aware of him as she sat stiffly in the back of the luxurious Cadillac, staring accusingly at him through her lashes as he stared back with narrowed eyes.

'Any good ideas where we can eat?' he asked, brows lifted.

'The Flaxton Table does a very nice supper,' she said shakily, not understanding his interest in her, yet at the same time understanding it at a deep level that terrified her.

They ate at the small family restaurant in the main street of the village. All the villagers, of course, knew what was happening at the manor, and gave her excited looks as she arrived with the American shark with the dark good looks and air of power.

Serena felt so gauche and unsophisticated in his presence. Twice she dropped her fork, and once she spilt the glass of orange juice he brought her.

'I hear you've only just left finishing school.' Nick Colterne watched her with narrowed speculative eyes. 'That makes you twenty—right?'

'Yes.' Serena found herself tongue-tied in his presence, her pulses racing as she stared again and again at his ruthless mouth and wondered how it would feel if he kissed her with it, very forcefully…very forcefully indeed.

'You're very beautiful,' he said softly, making her hand shake as his blue eyes burned into her. 'Any boyfriends?'

Serena laughed and shook her head. 'I haven't even met any boys yet. Except Derry, the gardener's son, and he's just silly.'

Nick's mouth hardened into a cynical smile, his eyes slipping to her breasts. 'Well,' he said under his breath, 'that's nice and clear.'

It was as though she had told him something important without realising it, and Serena just stared at him, her eyes wide as she tried to understand it.

When they drove home to Flaxton Manor, he held her wrist in the back of the car as she tried to open the door, and his blue eyes watched her with a look of dark sexual power that made her shake.

'Did you enjoy our evening?' he asked softly.

'Yes…' Serena said, mouth quivering as she stared at the tough face. 'Very much.'

His black lashes flickered on razor-sharp cheekbones. 'Do me a favour,' he said. 'When I come to close this deal tomorrow, put on that creamy lace dress you were wearing yesterday.'

Serena was surprised. She had bought the lace dress

from a second-hand shop last year for next to nothing. It fell in soft drapery over her slender curves, as elegant as it was clinging. 'The lace dress…? But why?'

'Just put it on,' he said with a hard twist to his mouth, his eyes rueful. 'As a little favour for me. I didn't get to see it properly. You were standing at the window—remember?'

'OK,' Serena said, her voice husky, not understanding but feeling very excited by the way he looked at her, spoke to her.

He smiled slowly, released her wrist. 'Tell your parents I'll arrive at eight tomorrow morning. I have to fly back to New York in the afternoon. Either we sign tomorrow or forget it.' His eyes watched her oddly. 'Will you tell them that, Lady Serena?'

She nodded, and left the car, trembling as she walked in and found her anxious parents hovering in the hall, waiting for her.

Serena told them what Nick Colterne had said.

'Sign tomorrow?' Her father frowned. 'That's rushing things a little, isn't it?'

'What does it matter, dear?' Her mother sighed, fingering her fake pearls. 'We're not in a position to be proud and he knows it. We need his money and his help. The faster we get it, the better. We'll just catch the tail end of the summer tourist trade if we open quickly.'

So the next morning Nick Colterne came back with his henchmen, his Cadillac and his air of power. Heart thudding, Serena watched him arrive, hidden from view behind the Elizabethan window-frames.

She put on her cream lace dress, combed out her

waist-length red hair and wondered why he wanted to see her in this. It was a very English design, the lace fragile, the cream silk below it skimming her womanly curves with elegance, ending in soft folds just below the knee.

Studying herself in the mirror, she thought of Nick Colterne and her green eyes darkened, her lips parting as she turned this way and that, suddenly feeling sensual, as though her skin was made of silk and her lips of velvet.

It was nine o'clock when she was called to the drawing-room.

Going in, she was surprised to find Nick Colterne alone. The sight of him made her heart thud with excitement, and she looked around for her parents with a frown.

Nick watched her intently, his ruthless eyes moving swiftly, restlessly over her body, stark sexual desire stamped on his tough face as he inspected her from head to foot.

He expelled his breath in an odd, hoarse, shaking way as he looked at her, and it made her quiver, staring through her lashes at his hard mouth.

'Come in, Lady Serena,' Nick said softly, a strange expression on his hard face. 'And close the door. I want to talk to you.'

Obediently, she did as she was told, her hands damp suddenly as she fidgeted with the folds of the dress, looking up at Nick hotly through her lashes.

He walked towards her, and said deeply, 'I don't have much time. I want to sign this deal and get the

wheels moving on it. But there's an essential ingredient in the package that I don't yet have.'

'I don't understand,' she said huskily.

'Yes, you do,' he said thickly, watching her.

Her eyes darted up to his and a slow flush crept over
her face.

Nick suddenly lifted his strong hands to her face,
making her gasp, staring up at him as he said under
his breath, 'You're the essential ingredient, Lady
Serena. You. That's why I've asked you here now. I'm
prepared to invest millions in Flaxton Manor—but
only on one condition.' His blue eyes slipped to her
mouth as he said, 'That you agree to be my wife.'

Serena whitened with shock, saying, 'You can't be
serious—'

'Deadly serious,' he said with a brief, cynical smile.
'Now, what's your answer? Will you marry me, yes
or no?'

'No!' she burst out at once, taking a step back, shaking with disbelief. 'You must be mad! Of course I
won't marry you! You're much older than me and—'

'I'm ten years older than you,' he drawled, his face
hardening with ruthless amusement. 'I'm thirty.'

'Well, I couldn't marry you even if you were
younger!' she said hoarsely, incredulous that he could
even ask. 'It's just ridiculous!'

His mouth hardened, a stain of dark red colouring
his face. 'I don't see that it's ridiculous,' he said
harshly, stepping away from her, running a hand
through his dark hair. 'It makes good business sense
to me.'

'How can it?'

'I want a wife who will give me an heir,' he said flatly, lifting his dark head, every inch the ruthless financial shark as he studied her with hard, narrowed blue eyes. 'But I've always wanted the best, and you're it. You're young, beautiful, titled…you're an heiress, an aristocrat and you're a virgin.'

'Oh…!' Serena caught her breath, a hand to her mouth, appalled as hot colour flooded her cheeks, and she turned away, saying hoarsely, 'Oh, my God…this is a nightmare!'

'Nightmare!' he bit out harshly behind her, striding up and catching her by the shoulder, whirling her angrily to face him, his blue eyes blazing. 'I'm offering to save your family from bankruptcy and ruin!'

'And ruining my life in the process!' she cried hoarsely.

His mouth tightened angrily. 'It's too late now! I've had it written into the contracts and they've got to be signed today!' He stared at her, then looked away, running a hand through his black hair. 'God! It never occurred to me that you'd refuse to—'

'Wait!' Serena said shakily, running to him, catching his arm, staring up into his face, her green eyes luminous. 'We'll be ruined if those contracts aren't signed.'

He looked at her sharply, his eyes narrowing, and there was a brief, tense silence. 'Do you like me, Lady Serena?' he asked softly, studying her face. 'Or is it all my imagination?'

She looked at his mouth and whispered, 'Yes…I do like you.'

His lashes flickered for a moment. Then he said

flatly, 'The contract will go through as written. We'll marry in one month from now. Your parents will have all the money they need to save the manor.'

'You talk as though it's already settled...' she said, horrified.

'It is,' he said bluntly. 'All I need is your acceptance, and we can get the wheels in motion.'

'And if I refuse?'

'Then the deal is off,' he said brutally.

Serena just stared at him, appalled. It was a gun to her head and they both knew it. If she refused to marry him, her family faced ruin. How could she possibly allow that to happen?

'You're blackmailing me!' she whispered bitterly, hot tears in her eyes.

He grimaced, saying thickly, 'I know. But I don't have time to do anything else. Now what's your answer, Lady Serena? Yes or no?'

Her hands twisted in despair. 'You know very well that I can't refuse!'

'Yes,' he said deeply, and walked towards her.

In her anger, she did not back away, instead staring at him bitterly as she felt her pulses race at his approach, hating him for the position he was putting her in.

'I'll make you happy,' he said under his breath as his hands slid to her waist, and his eyes to her mouth. 'I promise you that. You'll have everything you need. Now, send your parents back in. They're waiting for you in the library.'

Serena went with a thudding heart to find her parents. They were white with horror, and told her she

didn't have to marry him if she didn't want to. They
would face ruin, they said, for her sake. But of course
Serena knew she couldn't allow that to happen.

A month later, she was married to Nick Colterne
and had flown to the Bahamas for her honeymoon.

He came to her bedroom that night. Serena was
waiting for him, sitting up in bed, her face white as
porcelain, determination in her green eyes.

Nick closed the bedroom door behind him, studying
her across the darkness. He was wearing a dark red
dressing-gown, naked beneath it, his bronzed chest
bared and his long muscular thighs hair-roughened.
The sight of him made her pulses leap, but she hated
him for his ruthless acquisition of her and was determined not to let him make love to her.

The silence stretched tautly between them. Then
Nick pushed away from the door, walking slowly
across the darkened bedroom until he stood beside the
bed, staring down at Serena, his eyes hot blue.

'You're lovely,' he said abruptly, his voice hoarse.

Resentment flashed in her eyes. 'I suppose I ought
to be, considering how much money you paid to get
me.'

'Let's not discuss money in the bedroom,' he
drawled, sinking down on to the bed, making her
pulses leap with angry awareness as he reached for her.
'It's hardly good taste.'

'And what is good taste?' she demanded, backing
away from him until her head was pressed hard against
the expensive bedstead. 'Buying a wife for her title
and her inheritance?'

'I said we wouldn't discuss it,' he said softly, and

his hands reached for her, closing over her bare shoulders.

Rigid, Serena flung angrily, 'Don't touch me!'

His eyes narrowed. 'You're my wife. This is my wedding night. I have every right to touch you, and I damn well intend to. Now come here.' He pulled her towards him.

'No!' Serena struggled, hands splayed on his warm bronzed chest, excitement flashing through her as she encountered the black hairs that curled on his chest, angrily aware that she felt desire for him, and despising herself for it.

The blue eyes blazed. 'Yes!' he said thickly, and then his mouth closed over hers.

With a startled moan, she felt her mouth open beneath his, the hot exploration of his kiss exciting her at once. But her mind overruled her desire for him. He didn't love her. He only wanted an heir. That was all this was...business, not pleasure.

'Oh, God, I think I'm going to be sick!' Serena flung fiercely, dragging her mouth from his at once. 'I can't bear to have you anywhere near me!'

His eyes flashed angry blue. Pinning her to the bed, he kissed her deeply, ruthlessly, his mouth brutal over hers, and Serena was so furious that she felt something snap inside her, turning into a whirlwind, hands slapping and scratching at his face as he tried to capture her wrists and she screamed when he swore.

They fought in bitter silence. His eyes were blazing, his face dark red with anger. Then her fingernails raked his hard cheek, and his head jerked back.

Serena stared, breathing hard, as she saw blood on

his cheek. Slowly, he lifted a strong hand, touched the cut, then stared at the blood on his long fingers.

'I didn't mean to do that,' Serena said shakily. 'But I had to. I won't let you make love to me, Mr Colterne, marriage or no marriage. You're a stranger to me. Not a husband. And you'll never become my lover. Not unless you tie me down and rape me.'

He was suddenly very silent and very still, his harsh breathing the only sound in the darkened bedroom. His eyes glittered like blue fire. His anger was a tangible force, the tension crackling between them as he studied her, that long scratch on his cheek evidence of her determination, and the blood seemed to symbolise the catastrophic nature of their relationship.

Suddenly, he thrust her roughly from him. 'Fine,' he said tightly, getting to his feet. 'I've never made love to a woman who didn't want me and I don't intend to start now.'

Relief and acute disappointment swamped her as she lay very still, staring up at him.

'There have always been plenty of women ready to submit to me,' he drawled cruelly, watching her with a hard smile. 'There always will be. And I'll enjoy making love to them, Serena, until you decide you want to join their number.'

She gasped in outraged disbelief. 'Not until the day I die, you arrogant swine!'

'Men who are successful with women are always arrogant,' he said with a cold lift of his brows. 'I'm no different. Why should I put up with rejection from a spoilt little girl when I could have a warm, willing woman to share my bed?' He lifted his dark head, face very hard. 'Think about it, Serena. Perhaps you'll have changed your mind by morning.'

He turned, striding out of the bedroom without another word, and as the door slammed behind him Serena was already struggling with hot, bitter tears as she faced the reality of her marriage.

At breakfast the next morning, Nick was hostile to her.

'Thought about what I said last night?' he asked flatly as they sat tensely together on the sunlit patio overlooking the beach.

'Yes,' Serena said icily. 'And my answer is a resounding no. I wouldn't let you make love to me if you went down on your knees and begged me to!'

'Most unlikely,' he drawled tightly. 'As I believe I made clear last night, where women are concerned, I'm never the one who has to beg.'

Hot colour flooded her angry face. 'Oh, yes, I'm sure they're all throwing themselves at your feet, Mr Colterne. You're a very rich man and no doubt many women find you irresistible. I just don't happen to be one of them.'

'Then we're at a stalemate.' His eyes narrowed. 'For the moment. But it's not a stalemate I intend to live with forever, Serena. One clause in our marital contract was that you provide me with an heir.'

At that she paled, falling silent.

Nick studied her, mouth a cool line. 'Obviously, you're too young to consider living up to your side of the deal just yet. But you won't always be, Serena. Sooner or later, you've got to give me children, and we both know it.'

She swallowed, her throat dry as ashes. 'So you will inflict yourself on me? Whether I like it or not?'

'Oh, you'll like it,' he said softly, and watched the angry glitter of her green eyes before drawling, 'But we'll discuss it at a later date. In a few years' time. When you've grown up a bit. You'll see things differently then. You'll also have had time to live with frustration—' a ruthless smile curved his mouth as he said under his breath '—and you'll be very willing to end it.'

'Don't count on it!' she said bitterly, hating him.

He laughed softly, then got to his feet, a frown on his brow. 'In the meantime, though, we're going to have to deal with our incompatibility.'

She watched him in silence, the warm breeze lifting her red-gold hair.

'I'll keep mistresses,' Nick said coolly. 'I will, of course, keep them away from you. You'll never be humiliated publicly, you can rest assured of that. I have four homes—in New York, London, Hong Kong and this one here in Nassau.' He lifted dark brows. 'I'll hire a private secretary for you. She'll type out our schedules every month and we'll exchange them. That way, we need never bump into one another unless we have to.'

'Some marriage,' she said thickly, hating him.

'I married you for your title and your inheritance, Serena,' he drawled sardonically. 'I can get sex and female company elsewhere. I don't actually need them from you.'

Bitterly, she surveyed him. 'And we'll discuss children later?'

'Much later,' he said coolly.

Staring at the sun on the sea across the white sands of Nassau, Serena felt a quiver of fear. 'How much later?'

'When I think you're ready,' he said flatly, and walked away off the patio without another word.

So they had slipped into the routine of their marriage. It had worked, too. Serena had found herself left to live her own life as she wished, with all the money she could have dreamed of at her disposal, while Nick went his own way.

Occasionally, they would meet up at Flaxton Manor, putting on a brave show for her parents, who were anxious that Serena be happy. So she and Nick laughed and kissed for their benefit, and then went their separate ways again. Sometimes they had to go to Boston to see Nick's parents, and that was easier, because that Bostonian palace they lived in held no bitter memories for her.

Flaxton Manor had been opened to the public, become a successful tourist attraction, and over the following three years had gone from strength to strength, developing a garden centre in the grounds which her father doted on, and which had given him a new lease of life.

Now, however, Nick had suddenly appeared without warning and got into her bed, eliciting that swift, hot rush of pleasure and making Serena feel unaccountably afraid.

Lying in bed, staring at the lights of New York outside her window, she felt that fear grow deep inside her.

Was it true that his jet had been diverted? Was it true that this was an unplanned visit? Was it true that he would be leaving in the morning?

Or were his motives altogether—more sinister?

CHAPTER TWO

THE rattle of china woke Serena next morning. Lids flickering open sleepily, she frowned, wondering who it was. Then she remembered Nick and her body jackknifed into a sitting position. Heart thudding, she sat there, acutely aware of every movement he made in the kitchen. Her eyes flashed to the clock. Nine a.m. What was he still doing here?

Getting up, she went into the bathroom, washed her face and cleaned her teeth, wondering whether or not she should join him for breakfast. If she didn't, he might very well join her. A flush stained her cheeks at the memory of his kiss last night. She didn't want a repetition of that. There was no option but to go and join him and find out what his plans were.

She had planned to dress, but she heard him moving about outside her door, so she quickly snatched up her black négligé and shouldered into it with jerky movements, her heart skipping as she buttoned up the front of it with shaky fingers.

Wrenching open the door, she saw him with newspapers in his hand, strolling lazily past her.

He stopped, dangerously tall and sexy in his dark red pyjama trousers and bare chest. 'Morning,' he said coolly, flicking his blue eyes over her. 'I didn't know you'd added the *New York Artist* to our delivery list.'

Her eyes darted to the papers he held. 'I ordered it months ago...'

'You're paying for it yourself, too,' he noted with a wry movement of his dark brows. 'Out of your allowance. Or I would have noticed it on the bills.'

Stiffening, she said, 'Is it a crime, Nick?'

'No.' The dark brows drew together in a frown. 'Just secretive of you.'

'Everyone has secrets,' she said coolly.

He studied her for a moment, then walked away, his face unreadable. Serena watched him go, dry-mouthed. Damn! If she had known he was going to be here she would have telephoned the newsagents to cancel that order. She didn't like Nick's knowing anything about her life.

As she joined him in the kitchen she saw him lounging at the long pine table, drinking coffee and reading the *New York Post*. His bare chest was dangerously attractive, those broad shoulders tanned and powerfully muscled, black hair covering his chest to the long dark line at his navel.

'Can't you put something on?' Serena asked tautly, averting her gaze. 'You shouldn't wander around like that!'

His blue eyes flicked to hers. 'Why shouldn't I? It's my home.'

'Yes, but I'm here,' she said, folding her arms and hovering in the doorway at a distance from him.

He gave a cool laugh. 'You're my wife, Serena. You've seen my chest before!'

'Not very often!'

'That can easily be remedied,' he said softly, blue eyes mocking her as they slid with insolent sexual appraisal over her slender body.

'Very funny, Nick!' she said tightly, green eyes flashing at him. 'Now, please put something on, or I'll have to eat breakfast in the living-room.'

There was a tense little silence. Nick studied her through narrowed eyes, then said softly, 'You didn't blush. Perhaps you are growing up, after all.'

Hot colour swept her cheeks immediately and she turned to walk away from the door, hating him for having made her so acutely aware of him, and making her feel a fool because of it.

The soft laughter that came from the kitchen made her grind her teeth with rage. She heard him walk coolly out, go into his bedroom, and get his dressing-gown.

'There,' he drawled lazily, presenting himself in his dark red dressing-gown, hands thrust deeply in the pockets. 'Am I now fit for breakfasting with?'

Serena studied him through her gold lashes. 'Yes, of course,' she said, recovering herself with dignity, and followed him into the kitchen, realising with a sudden shock that after three years of marriage her husband was almost a stranger to her.

And a very disturbing stranger, at that.

He sank down in his chair again, flicked open the *Post*, and began reading.

Serena studied his hard profile. A ruthless tycoon who had married her for her title and inheritance... why did he insist on keeping their marriage going when it was such a shell? Why did she? A sigh left her full mouth, and she cleared her throat.

'When do you leave for Washington?'

'Washington?' he drawled, his American accent giving the capital city an air of glamour.

'Yes,' she said coolly, walking to the table and deliberately lowering his newspaper with one slim hand, meeting the sudden steely flick of his eyes. 'Washington! You remember. You were on your way there last night!'

He studied her for a second. 'You're getting bold, Serena.'

She lifted her chin. 'I don't want you here, Nick. I made that plain last night.'

'That's not all you made plain,' he said softly, mockingly, and let his eyes drift to her mouth. 'That was quite a kiss you gave me in bed. I almost thought I'd got the wrong apartment.'

Hot colour swept over her face. 'I was asleep!' she said accusingly. 'I didn't know what was happening!'

'Neither did I,' he said lazily. 'I expected you to start screaming as soon as I touched you and try to claw my eyes out. That's your usual response to my touch, isn't it?' His eyes narrowed speculatively. 'I wonder what made last night different.'

'I just told you,' Serena said flatly, turning away to get a plate and cup from the cupboard, refusing to look at him any more in case he saw the flare of sudden arousal in her green eyes. 'I was asleep and I didn't know what was happening. I was having a dream, if you must know. That's why I woke up so slowly...

why it took so long for me to realise what you were doing.'

He smiled sardonically, drawling, 'Nothing to do with me personally, then?'

'No!' she said angrily, sitting down and reaching for the coffee-pot. 'You know perfectly well how I feel about you personally.'

'Oh, yes,' he said softly, mockingly. 'I disgust you. Sure. It came across loud and clear last night!'

Her green eyes burned with angry accusation. 'It must have done, or you would never have left me alone, Nick!'

His mouth curved in a cynical smile. 'Well, maybe I have other plans for you,' he said softly. 'Later on in the day...' He shook out the *New York Post*, cynical blue eyes flicking over the small newsprint again.

Serena ignored him, and buttered a slice of toast, but inside she was shaken. This argument was too personal. His kiss last night had been too personal. In fact—everything so far about this little 'visit' was too personal.

They had got through the last three years without ever having personal conversations. Normally, they were polite strangers with very little to say to each other. The arrangement worked very well. Why was Nick suddenly tampering with it? Flicking a series of switches and provoking personal confrontation...?

Because he's got nothing better to do, she thought bitterly. He lived life at a whirlwind pace, blasting his way through obstacles, rarely stopping to think of the consequences of his actions on the people he blasted out of his way.

Odd that he should operate like that, given his family background. His parents were wealthy Bostonian bankers. Nick had been born into a world of American grace and privilege, and had not quite fitted in. His dynamic personality and quick, enquiring mind had stuck out like a sore thumb in that world.

But, although their strange marriage had given her brief glimpses into his past, she was aware that their conversations never turned to personal subjects.

Like sex, for instance, she thought with a prickle of unease.

Nick had opened this visit with sex, and the subject was still lingering between them like a crackle of electricity, making Serena distinctly nervous.

Shooting him an anxious look, she said huskily, 'Nick, you are leaving this morning, aren't you?'

He didn't look at her. 'I'll be leaving just as soon as the jet's ready. The pilot's going to call me.'

'Oh…' She nodded, bit into her toast with small white teeth.

Serena wanted him out of the apartment as soon as possible. Tomorrow was a big day for her. She didn't want Nick complicating it. His presence here today was unexpected and unwelcome, but at least it wouldn't blow a hole in her private life. Whereas tomorrow…

Suddenly Nick got to his feet. 'I'm going to take a shower and get dressed,' he announced, throwing the newspaper on to the table. 'If the pilot rings, take a message for me.'

He strode out of the room, leaving her burning with resentment. He treated her like his secretary. Well, not quite, she thought with a flash of anger towards him, because he was probably having an affair with his secretary.

Clearing the table, Serena put the dishes in the dishwasher. The luxury apartment block on Fifth Avenue was kept in perfect order by the people who ran it. There were no personal staff here, although all Nick's other homes did have personal staff.

This was one of her favourite homes. Nick had excellent taste, and all his homes were furnished in a similar style with French antiques, pale green or cream and gold colours, and a general air of Bostonian elegance. It appealed to her sense of beauty, and was in keeping with her love of 'old money' as opposed to flashy new. Her own family background was not as luxurious or stylish as Nick's, but she had often wished it were. The threadbare, faded beauty of Flaxton Manor had been charming, but hard to live with, particularly when springs leapt out of ancient sofas and cut one's legs, or whole sections of roof caved in after rainfall.

Serena went to her bedroom and took a delicious shower. With wet hair, she wrapped a cream towelling robe around her slender body and padded into the bedroom.

It would be a good idea to hide her paintings from Nick in case he saw them. The last thing she wanted was for him to find out she was flourishing as an artist behind his back.

Going to her wardrobe, she opened it, then picked up the packing cases crammed with her numerous paintings, and lugged them into the wardrobe with a

groan. The canvases were very heavy. She locked the
door and went to her dressing-table to blow-dry her
hair.

Later, she strolled into the living-room in a peacock-
blue silk shift dress, her long red-gold hair in her usual
style, falling seductively over one eye.

She looked at the telephone and frowned. It was
ominously silent. Was Nick really diverted here unexpectedly? His fleet of air staff was usually so efficient. If there was something wrong with the jet…

Nick's bedroom door burst open and he strode in.
'I'm bored!' he announced in that cool Bostonian
voice, running a hand through his freshly washed black
hair, devastatingly attractive in a blue-grey business
suit, every inch the powerful, sexy tycoon. 'I don't
want to sit around here all day waiting for a call! Let's
go out!'

'Out?' Serena repeated, staring.

'Sure. Why not?' He strode to the telephone and
switched on the answering machine with long, quick
fingers. 'Do some shopping, have some lunch.'

Her lips parted. 'But we never go out together…'

'Don't we?' He straightened, face cynical. 'I never
noticed.'

'You're always too busy being Nick Colterne to notice,' she said with a haughty flick of her lashes, then,
'Anyway—what about the jet? If they call—'

'They can leave a message like everybody else,' he
drawled, and ran his insolent blue eyes over her slender curves. 'I like the dress. Very sexy. Needs some
shoes, though. Go and put them on and let's get out
of here.'

Serena's mouth tightened. 'Don't order me about, Nick!'

'Why not?' he drawled, a sardonic smile on his hard mouth.

'Because I don't like it!' she snapped, hating him with a sudden fierce passion.

'Well, isn't that just too bad?' he drawled softly, a mocking smile on his ruthless mouth as he studied her, challenging her to do what she suddenly realised she wanted to do: slap his cynical face and wipe that smile right off it.

Their eyes warred in a moment of hair-raising electricity. Then Serena tightened her lips and stormed into her bedroom, trembling with rage, to fling open her walk-in wardrobe and get her high heels, jamming them on her feet in a burst of uncharacteristic fury.

'Don't slam about, beautiful!' Nick drawled from the doorway, leaning there, hands in trouser pockets, watching her with mockery, and she turned, eyes flashing wide with sudden fear in case he moved into the room and saw the tell-tale packing cases.

'So sorry, Nick,' she said sweetly, and closed the doors of the walk-in wardrobe. She locked the doors.

Nick watched with narrowed eyes. 'Why are you locking the doors?'

'Just a habit.' She smiled at him, watching him through her gilt-tipped lashes.

His lashes flickered on razor-sharp cheekbones. 'Not hiding your lover in there, I hope?' he murmured, and suddenly the mockery was gone from his face, the ruthless cut-throat shark sending waves of excited fear through her.

'We don't all live like you, Nick,' Serena said with cold contempt. 'We don't all indulge our carnal desires with impunity!'

He laughed softly, blue eyes insolent as they roved to her breasts. 'Carnal desires? Now there's an interesting phrase...'

That look took her breath away, made her veins pulse with sudden fierce heat, and she hated him for it, hated his stark sexual appetite and the ruthlessness with which he indulged it.

'I thought we were going out!' she snapped, furious to find she was almost trembling as his blue eyes moved lazily, cynically over her body, taking in the narrow waist and the sensual curve of her hips, so seductive in the peacock-blue silk shift dress.

He straightened, bored with toying with her. 'Sure. Come on. Let's hit Manhattan and buy a few stores.'

They went down in the luxurious lift. Nick was coolly indifferent to her, jingling change in his pockets, eyes narrowed in thought. Serena stood beside him, feeling superfluous, as she always did, and hating him.

New York was in the grip of this heat wave, and the sun blazed down on the city that was a living twentieth-century masterpiece of modern art, its jagged spires piercing a hot blue sky, its pavements moneyed and fast-paced. It was the Oxford of ambition.

'Hi, Mr Colterne!' The doorman saluted cheerily. 'Lady Serena!'

'Hi!' Nick strode by him like a whirlwind. The chauffeur opened the limousine door. Nick got into the luxurious rear. All very fast, very smooth. Nick didn't have to alter his stride once.

Serena slid in beside him. The door shut. Her green eyes surveyed his tough profile in the back of the limousine as he looked at his watch, the crisp white cuffs shooting back, the Rolex glittering on his hair-roughened wrist.

'Eleven,' he said flatly. 'Take us to Faulke's.'

The chauffeur pulled away with a smooth surge of power. Serena glanced out of the window. She adored New York. The pace, the cosmopolitan atmosphere, the stark steel skyscrapers and the elegance of the older establishments.

Nick prowled around Faulke's, ordering things left, right and centre. Saleswomen followed him with admiration, fluttering their eyelashes while he cynically inspected their red mouths and slim bodies. Serena watched him operate, hatred in her eyes.

They had lunch at the Plaza. Heads turned as they walked in. Waiters swarmed all over them, and Nick dismissed them with a curt wave of his hand, striding across the restaurant with Serena behind him.

'We haven't done this in a long time,' Nick observed as they sat at the elegant table drinking Château Lafite and waiting for their main course. 'When did I last bump into you, anyway?'

'Christmas,' she said flatly. 'At Flaxton Manor.'

'That's right. And it's June now.'

'How the months drift by,' she said, disliking him intensely.

'Do they drift by, Serena?' he asked with a cool lift

of dark brows. 'Or are they beginning to speed up for
you lately?'

She tensed, watching him with sudden wariness.
'Speed up? Why should they speed up?'

A slow, sardonic smile touched his hard mouth.
'Well, now, they might one day. You never know.
After all—you can't spend the rest of your life flying
aimlessly around the world with nothing to do and no
lover to make—'

'I do wish you'd try to be polite!' she said tightly,
green eyes flashing as she cut into his insulting sentence midstream. 'It's bad enough having you here
without warning, without having to put up with your
bad manners too!'

His face tightened into a hard mask. 'Don't speak
to me like that, Serena,' he said, his blue eyes suddenly
as ruthless as his steel-edged tone.

'Or what?' she challenged suddenly, although her
blood pulsed in fierce, unexpected response to the look
in his eyes, and her voice was unsteady, threaded with
sudden desire to provoke.

'Or I'll take you home and take you to bed,' he said
under his breath, menace lacing his voice, his mouth
very hard. 'How's that for a threat?'

She was breathless, her lips parted and her breathing
erratic.

'Good girl,' he murmured, hard mouth curving with
a cynical smile. 'Now—tell me what you've been up
to since Christmas at Flaxton Manor. I feel I ought to
have some idea of my wife's activities.'

'As if you care!' she said thickly, loathing him intensely. 'You only married me for my title and my

inheritance. I could die tomorrow and you wouldn't care.'

'Hardly,' he drawled. 'We don't have any children yet, so nobody would inherit a damned thing.'

'You know what I mean!' she said angrily.

He laughed under his breath, watching her with steely eyes. 'Why do I get the feeling you're trying to avoid answering any of my questions?'

That made her catch her breath and look at him closely, deeply aware of that ruthless mind and the speed at which it moved. Her heart was thumping unsteadily and she realised she was under threat of exposure if she didn't tread very carefully indeed.

'Ask anything you want,' she said with a sudden, curving smile.

His dark lashes flickered. He was coolly amused. 'A dutiful wife,' he mocked.

Their main course arrived at that moment, ending the conversation, to her relief. Her sole was delicious, light and very fresh, served with crisp vegetables. Nick ate steak tartare, one of his favourite dishes, and typically Nick, all that blood and raw meat.

'So what do you do in your spare time these days, Serena?' Nick deftly swung that lethal weapon back on her as they drank coffee. 'You have so much of it. You must do something.'

She gave him a sweet smile. 'I have cocktail parties, see people for dinner.'

'Ring-a-ding-ding!' drawled Nick sarcastically.

'I like being lazy,' she said coolly. 'We don't all have to run around the world axing people to bits and making billions of dollars.'

'I don't axe people to bits,' he said flatly. 'And
without my billions of dollars, your precious manor
would have gone to the wall. Remember that, next
time you start levelling criticism at me.'

'How could I forget?' Serena said tightly. 'You
bought me along with the manor, and ruined my life!'

He gave a dangerous smile, drawling, 'Well, honey,
you sure weren't worth the price!' and her face went
white with appalled realisation of how painful their
marriage could become if they ever spent too much
time together.

Suddenly, Monique Dupré was advancing on their
table, ravishing in flame-red, her bony face and even
bonier body those of an ex-model, now moved on to
become the art critic of one of the quality New York
papers.

Serena stiffened with jealousy and dislike. Her eyes
flashed back to Nick's tough face. Monique was one
of his mistresses. She didn't know how many he had,
but she knew she would hate every one of them as
much as she hated Monique.

'Nick, darling!' Monique purred, sliding red-taloned
fingers over his powerful shoulders. 'I didn't know you
were in town.'

'Surprise visit,' drawled Nick, standing up, cynical
eyes on her red mouth as he bent his dark head and
kissed it.

Searing jealousy flooded Serena's veins like acid.
Bitterly, she looked the other way. What else could
she do?

'Lady Serena,' Monique said politely, noticing her
white, tense face. 'Long time no see.'

Serena looked at her with angry dignity. 'Hello, Monique. How's the art world of Manhattan?'

'I would have thought you'd know more about that than me,' Monique said softly, her dark eyes watching Serena's face as colour flooded into it.

'What on earth makes you say that?' Serena said at once, her tone icy, then looked at Nick. 'We ought to be getting back. The pilot may have called. Or don't you want to leave now?'

There was a brief silence. Nick studied her with narrowed eyes, then said briskly, 'Sure. You're right.' He beckoned a waiter with one hand, and stroked Monique's bony cheek with the other. 'I'll give you a call, Monique. Take care.'

The limousine took them back to Fifth Avenue and their apartment. Serena prayed there would be a message on the answering machine. The sooner Nick left, the better.

As they walked into the apartment Nick said curtly, 'Get me my schedule, would you, Serena? It's in my bedroom, on the dresser.' He strode to the answering machine, bending his dark head.

Serena tightened her mouth, hating the way he was suddenly ordering her around as though she were an employee. He'd never done it before. Had three years of this empty marriage made him despise her?

Her hands shook as she picked up his schedule and examined it. If Nick despised her...she couldn't bear to think of it. The pain it aroused was too deep, too unfamiliar, too unexpected to cope with.

'Any message?' Serena asked flatly as she walked back into the living-room.

'Yes,' he said coolly, erasing the tape. 'The jet's going to be out of action for another twenty-four hours.'

Serena stopped, frowning, staring at him. 'But that's ridiculous…'

'These things happen.' He shrugged.

She stared at the answering machine. Her lashes flickered. 'Why are you erasing the tape, Nick?'

There was a little silence. He looked at her, his face cool. 'It was full. You must get a lot of calls.'

Serena tapped the schedule in her hands thoughtfully. 'Not that many.'

He swung away from her, striding to the drinks cabinet. 'At any rate, I'll have to stay another night.'

Her heart stopped beating at the prospect and she heard her voice say in an odd, hoarse note, 'I don't want you here, Nick. Please don't stay.'

'It's my apartment,' he drawled, unscrewing a bottle of whisky. 'I can do what I like.'

Her mouth tightened. 'We agreed a long time ago that we would live separate lives!'

'And we do.' He poured a small measure of whisky. 'Come on, Serena. I'm not that bad. We can surely spend one night together without this kind of row.'

She moistened her lips, her eyes racing over his powerful head, shoulders, the tapered hips and long muscular legs. He was so potently masculine, his sex appeal a tangible force that was like a rocket.

'You'll be leaving tomorrow?' she asked thickly. 'First thing in the morning?'

'First thing.' He turned, a hand thrust in the pocket

of that impeccably cut grey suit, legs apart in a stance of masculine authority that sent a quiver through her.

Breathless suddenly, she nodded her red-gold head. 'I suppose I can live with you until then.'

A tight smile hardened his ruthless mouth. 'How very kind of you to say so.' There was a biting edge to his voice that threatened an argument, and Serena suddenly knew it was imperative they get through this disastrous surprise visit without an argument.

They never argued. They never really saw each other, and when they did they were surrounded by relatives who managed to keep their relationship on a superficial, easygoing note as they talked like polite strangers and just got through the awful moments together.

'Well...' Serena put his schedule down on the telephone table, her eyes wary '...I'll just go and tidy my room. Perhaps I'll see you later.' Turning, she walked the very long, tense distance back to her bedroom, and closed the door quietly, leaning on it, breathing hard.

What on earth was she going to do? It was like being locked up with a stick of dynamite, and she was beginning to realise there was a lot more to his 'surprise' visit than met the eye.

But what? What...? Serena sat in her room alone for the rest of the afternoon, struggling to find an answer. Why would he come here out of the blue like this? What on earth did he want from her?

At seven she realised she couldn't stay in here forever or she would go slowly mad. Better to face the pacing tiger that was her husband than her own rapidly growing boredom and frustration.

Nick was in the dining-room, working. He looked up as she came in. Papers were scattered all over the elegant mahogany dining-table. The phone was next to him, his computer switched on and a calculator at his side.

'Yes?' he asked curtly as he saw her.

She pursed her full mouth. 'I'm bored.'

There was a brief silence. His blue gaze flicked over her and he sat back suddenly, a hard smile curving his cynical mouth. 'Oh…?'

'I thought I might go out,' she said, prickling against the swift excitement his gaze provoked so unexpectedly in her. 'See some friends.'

His smile faded, his mouth hardening as he tensed. 'I thought we could have dinner alone together to-night,' he said with a frown. 'I booked a table at Twenty-one.'

Serena swallowed, said huskily, 'We'll only argue, Nick. You must see that. We've been on the edge of a row since you arrived.'

'We've been on the edge, all right,' he said under his breath, a hard look in his eyes, and she responded to that look without warning, her heart skipping beats and her body flooding with hot excitement.

'I won't spend any more time in your company than I have to!' she said more fiercely than she had meant to, and slammed the door, heard him leap up and come running after her, and quickly grabbed her handbag from the living-room, dashing out of the apartment.

He broke out of the front door like a whirlwind as she waited for the lift. 'What the hell are you playing at?' he bit out, striding towards her, blue eyes flashing with rage. 'You're my wife! If I want to have dinner with you, I damned well will!'

'I'm a human being!' she said hotly, jabbing the call button with a shaking hand. 'You can't—'

'Oh, can't I?' he said tightly, and took a ruthless stride towards her, grabbing her wrist and dragging her suddenly against his hard body. 'I bought you, I paid for you, and I can do what I like with you!'

The lift arrived.

'No!' Serena shouted hoarsely, shaking as she pushed at his broad shoulders and backed into the lift, green eyes blazing with rage. 'You damned well can't!'

Their eyes clashed as she stood in the lift and he stood in the corridor. He was darkly flushed, breathing harshly, his mouth white with rage. So was Serena.

The lift doors slowly closed.

Leaning weakly against the wall, she felt close to tears. Their marriage was almost ready to smash to bits like deadwood on the rocks and the pain clawing at her stomach would not go away, no matter how much she told herself she hated him, no matter how bitter this had become, no matter how angry he made her with his ruthless, heartless words.

Serena went out on to the hot New York pavement, shaking.

How did we reach this point? she wondered, closing her eyes.

How...?

CHAPTER THREE

SERENA got back to the apartment at midnight. She had visited some friends in the upper eighties, but the evening had been ruined by her deep-running feelings about Nick and her fear over why he was here.

With trepidation, she opened the front door and went in, heart thudding, to find the apartment empty. The antique clock ticked on the mantelpiece. Beside it lay a note, telling her he had gone out for the evening.

With Monique, I bet, thought Serena bitterly, and crumpled up the note, shaking suddenly with such overwhelming jealousy and hatred that she almost burst into tears.

She went to bed and lay awake in agony until he came home at three in the morning. He bumped into a piece of furniture and she heard him swear under his breath.

His footsteps stopped outside her room. He tried the door, found it locked, and there was an electrifying silence. Serena could sense his rage as he stood outside the locked door. She could almost hear him breathing, thickly, almost see his blue eyes blazing. For a horrifying second she wondered if he would kick the door to splinters and crash in...

Then he walked away, slamming his bedroom door,

and she felt a flood of disappointment so violent that she was appalled. I don't want him to be anywhere near me, she thought, shaking. I hate him.

Next morning she woke early. Had Nick gone? She went into the living-room, found it silent, empty. His bedroom door was open. He had gone.

Pain clutched at her heart and she was baffled by her own reactions to him. She had wanted him to go—hadn't she? He was a bastard and she was well rid of him.

Phil was arriving at eleven-thirty for drinks and lunch. He was one of her newest friends, an American art dealer who was interested in her paintings. She had brought the latest stack of paintings from London to show him, and it was as well that Nick had left before Phil arrived.

Going into her bedroom again, Serena pushed Nick from her mind, took a shower and got dressed. At eleven-fifteen she was ready, her long red-gold hair a cascade of silken waves falling to her waist, green eyes slanting, full pink mouth emphasised with coral lipstick. The green silk shift dress skimmed her slender curves with sensual emphasis, and her high-heeled shoes were the final touch of gloss and sophistication that she had so gradually developed.

Nick was in the living-room when she went out. He stood by the mantelpiece, devastatingly attractive in a black business suit, a gold watch-chain glittering across his taut black waistcoat.

Whitening, sucking in her breath, Serena froze. 'What are you doing here?' she demanded hoarsely.

'I decided to stay,' he drawled with a hard smile,

hands thrust in black trouser-pockets, his ruthless air of power making her eyes race over his body with fierce, prickling attraction. 'Any objections?'

'You know perfectly well I don't want you here!'

'And I want to find out why,' he said, arching black brows at her.

Her heart hammered. Defensively, she said, 'Did you have a good time with your mistress last night?' Her green eyes flared. 'I heard you bumping into furniture at three in the morning!'

'Jealous, Serena?'

Hot colour flooded her face. 'Don't flatter yourself,' she said flatly, hating him. 'I'm delighted you have so many women. It keeps your disgusting attentions away from me!'

A muscle jerked in his cheek. 'Speaking of which, I'm afraid it's time I made a little confession. I've decided to stay on here with you for a purpose.'

Dry-mouthed, she said thickly, 'What purpose?' but her blood was racing and she knew…she knew from the way he had been looking at her…that special look, that ruthless sexual power in his eyes that told her he wanted her in the worst way, and suddenly she couldn't stand the tension any more. 'Your jet didn't break down, did it? You planned this surprise visit from start to finish! That's why you've been talking about sex, looking at me like that…'

'Think of our marriage as a business deal,' he drawled. 'And this is where you have to keep your side of the bargain.'

'Bargain!' she said bitterly. 'You can't talk about marriage like that, Nick, but you do! You always have done! That's why there was never a love-clause written into our contract!'

'What the hell is love?' Nick drawled with a ruthless smile.

She lowered her lashes, hating him.

'You're twenty-three,' he said, watching her with those penetrating blue eyes. 'And I'm now thirty-three. I want to be young enough to enjoy my children, Serena, and the clock is ticking fast.'

Her face was white. 'Is this a demand, Nick? Are you going to—enforce it if I refuse?'

'Force you to make love with me?' He slid those blue eyes over her body, smiling sardonically. 'An interesting idea. But I'd find it infinitely more exciting if you gave me a hot look, slid your dress off and said, Come to bed, sexy.'

She caught her breath, rage flooding her veins. 'My God, you bastard!'

'Sexy bastard,' he drawled, walking towards her. 'That would do the trick.'

Serena backed, heart hammering, and he caught her wrist.

'You can't get out of it again, Serena,' he said softly. 'I let you off the hook three years ago because you were twenty and obviously too young to handle it. But you're not twenty any more. And the way you kissed me the other night told me all I needed to know.'

'That's why you did it,' she whispered, staring at his ruthless mouth. 'You came here out of the blue at three in the morning with the express purpose of—'

'Turning you on,' he said under his breath, and her

legs felt suddenly weak, her lips parting, breathing erratically as she stared at him.

His strong hands were sliding to her waist. She started to push weakly at his broad shoulders, but he just smiled that hard smile, and his blue eyes dropped to her mouth.

'I need more time…!'

'You can't have it,' he said softly.

'What do you want me to do?' she asked rawly, her legs shaking beneath her as her hands fluttered weakly on his broad shoulders. 'Just go into the bedroom with you and—?'

'No. I think I'm going to take this one step at a time,' he said under his breath. 'And I'll enjoy every step, because I've wanted to see you lose control sexually for a long time, Serena.' His hands tightened on her waist, his dark head bending, hard mouth brushing against hers as he whispered, 'I've dreamt about it. I've prayed for it. I've spent years driving myself crazy with lust over—'

'I hate you!' she said, her mouth shaking. 'I hate you!'

A sardonic smile touched his mouth. 'Oh, I don't know about that,' he said softly, and leant towards her, his blue eyes moving in slow, leisurely inspection of her mouth, sliding down her taut white neck to the swell of her breasts beneath the green silk.

'Don't!' she said shakily. 'Don't look at me like that…!' She felt overpowered by the sexual threat he was imposing.

'Why not, Serena?' he asked with lazy sardonic

mockery, and ran one long finger over her quivering mouth. 'Does it disturb you?'

'Yes!' she whispered furiously, and he smiled, his dark head lowering slowly, his blue eyes terrifying her, and as his mouth closed over hers with hard authority she gave a quick cry of alarm, her hands instantly coming up to fight him, raining blows on his broad shoulders.

Nick took her hands, pinned them to her waist, and his kiss turned savage, making her open her mouth to him with a helpless little cry, forcing her to kiss him back as the blood began to drum in her ears.

He was kissing her with fierce desire, and she was struggling with hot moans of angry excitement, heart drumming, pushing at his shoulders uselessly, then at his chest, and all the time that savage mouth was claiming ownership, obliterating her helpless struggles until she was dragged into the dark sea of sexual excitement by his skill and experience.

Dizzy, she stood with her eyes closed, helpless beneath the onslaught of his kisses, her mouth opened to him in hot, untutored response. His strong hands slid slowly up her body, over her flat stomach, making her quiver and moan little refusals against his mouth until those hands closed over her breasts and she gave a long, hoarse cry.

Nick made a rough sound under his breath, his mouth increasing the pressure and his strong fingers dextrously stroking her erect nipples as she gasped in overwhelming excitement, unable to fight him or herself any longer, drowning in that dark sea of sexual hunger that he had so deliberately unleashed on her.

When he drew his head away she was shaking, gasping hoarsely, her mouth bruised with passion and her green eyes flickering open with a fierce glitter of excitement to stare at him.

'The doorbell,' Nick said thickly under his breath, a quick frown on his darkly flushed face as he released her. 'I'll get it.' He broke away from her, raking a hand through his thick black hair as he strode off towards the door.

Phil! Serena struggled back to reality, fear making her pale as she pushed shaking hands through her red-gold hair, appalled at what had just happened, and even more appalled at the thought of what Nick would think when Phil came in...

'Oh, I'm sorry...' Phil's voice in the expensive hall-way made her groan. 'I thought this was Lady Serena's apartment—'

'It is,' Nick's arrogant voice drawled flatly. 'I'm her husband. Who the hell are you?'

Serena was trembling, going to the luxurious hall of the apartment with a sinking heart just as Phil's startled voice said, 'Her husband!'

'Hello, Phil!' Serena tried to inject some good cheer into her voice, but it was ragged and her face was deeply flushed as she met Phil's astonished dark eyes. 'I'm sorry about this. I should have telephoned and let you know—'

'Let him know what?' Nick asked at once, turning to her, blue eyes sharply narrowed.

Her flush deepened. 'I had arranged to lunch with Phil, spend the day with him.'

'Darling,' Nick drawled in a dangerous voice, smiling at her with his teeth bared and his eyes narrowed, 'don't you think you should introduce me to your friend?'

Her heart skipped a beat. 'Yes, of course…ill-mannered of me…forgive me…' She swallowed convulsively, and turned to Phil. 'Phil Greyson. This is my husband, Nick Colterne. Nick—'

'How do you do?' Nick was towering over Phil, extending a strong tanned hand in a firm shake, his eyes hostile. 'My wife seems to think my presence makes your lunch impossible. I, on the other hand, do not. Won't you come in?'

Serena met Phil's eyes and saw the look of enquiry in their dark depths. She had told him nothing of her marriage. He had asked her questions about Nick, of course, because he was such a well-known figure in American society. Nick Colterne's wealth and power were as formidable a force as his personality. He had cachet in the eyes of most Americans, and his hard face was frequently in the gossip columns.

'Thank you,' Phil was saying, walking in with a smile, his blond hair smooth and his grey suit fashionably cut. 'I must say, it's a pleasure to meet you at last, sir! I've heard so much about you!'

'How charming!' Nick drawled, casting a steely look at Serena. 'I'm afraid I've heard absolutely nothing about you. Sit down, Mr Greyson! Let me get you a drink while you tell me all about yourself!'

'Thanks very much,' Phil said, smiling broadly as he sank into a pale gold armchair, obviously very much at home in the apartment. 'A gin and tonic would be lovely.'

Serena walked shakily into the room, sank on to the couch, watching Nick's hard body as he swung to the cocktail cabinet, opened the carved French wooden doors and began unscrewing the lid of a bottle of gin.

Why was he being so charming to Phil?

'What do you do, Greyson?' Nick asked, casting a cool glance over one broad shoulder. 'You don't look like a financier or—'

'I'm an art dealer,' Phil said with a smile, his New York accent at odds with the cool, clipped Bostonian drawl of Nick Colterne. 'I run the Vane Gallery on Park and Eighty-third.'

'Really?' Nick's eyes narrowed on Serena, who hurriedly averted her gaze, pretending to examine a speck of fluff on the couch. 'That must be a very interesting job. Tell me how you met my wife.' He turned, a hard smile on his mouth as he strolled arrogantly to Phil and handed him a tumbler of gin and tonic.

'Well, it was all very much a chapter of accidents.' Phil laughed, flicking an affectionate glance to Serena. 'She kept haunting the gallery, I noticed her, then she suddenly disappeared. A month later I went to London for an exhibition, and there she was.'

'How romantic!' Nick said in a dangerous voice, and shot a look at Serena through his black lashes that made her heart miss a beat.

'Well, it wasn't romantic!' Phil hurriedly assured him, flushing. 'But it did feel rather fated.'

'And when was this...fatalistic but unromantic meeting?' Nick drawled, with a smile like a lazy tiger.

'Last month,' Phil said with a flicker of dark lashes,

oblivious to the danger in Nick's voice. 'We've been friends ever since, haven't we, Lady Serena?'

Serena nodded warily, her eyes pinned on Nick.

'Well, I think that's very nice,' Nick said softly, examining his glass of whisky on ice. 'And I take it that, as such very good friends, you see each other at least every day....?'

'More or less,' Phil agreed, nodding. 'Except Lady Serena's just popped back to England to fetch these paintings for me. I haven't actually seen her since last week—I've been away, and—'

'Paintings?' Nick said, very softly.

Serena got to her feet, saying quickly, 'I'd better ring the Four Seasons and cancel lunch. I really don't think this is the time or the place for—'

'Cancel?' Phil stared at her. 'But you can't cancel!'

'I quite agree,' Nick drawled with a hard, sardonic smile as he flicked his lashes in Serena's direction. 'But do ring the Four Seasons, darling. And change the booking to a table for three. In my name.' He looked back at Phil with a lazy blue gleam in his eyes. 'My treat, Greyson. I insist...'

The Four Seasons was packed with the most fashionable New Yorkers, and the most startlingly avant-garde décor. Glittering bead curtains hung over thirty-foot windows. The heat wave outside was reflected within, as smart businesswomen normally in power suits seemed to have melted in the heat into soft, feminine creatures in floaty summer dresses and floral scents.

'Mr Colterne!' The *maître d'* bowed to Nick.

'Good afternoon,' Nick clipped out coolly, striding

up the steps with a nod, devastatingly authoritative as he turned, waited for Serena to join him and slid a strong hand to the small of her back as she reached him.

They were given the best table in the house. Serena felt the stares of other women as they passed. Nick always attracted attention from women. His height and rugged good looks were laced with a predatory sexual menace that most women found irresistible.

'Champagne,' Nick ordered coolly, flicking the wine list shut and handing it back to the *maître d'*. Turning to look at Serena, he drawled lazily, 'It seems to me this lunch is something of a celebration.' His smile was alarming. 'Is that correct?'

'Well, it should have been!' Phil said, laughing. 'I wanted it to be the close of a deal, but—'

'Shouldn't we study the menu?' Serena cut in hurriedly, desperate to keep the subject firmly away from her real reasons for this lunch.

'I know it by heart,' Nick said flatly with a warning look. 'And so should you. You eat here often enough.'

Her eyes widened. Nick obviously paid close attention to her expenses or he wouldn't know that.

Nick treated Phil to a slow, charming smile. 'What deal would you have been closing with my wife, Greyson?'

'It doesn't mat—' she began urgently.

'Well, the exhibition deal,' Phil said at exactly the same time.

There was a brief silence. Nick was staring at Serena, his face hard. Suddenly, his black lashes flickered.

'Exhibition…?' he asked softly, smiling.

'Phil, please…' Serena whispered under her breath, but he was already talking, and he didn't hear her.

'…such an accomplished artist!' Phil's dark eyes were alight. 'I was staggered when I saw her work. Of course, I haven't seen all of it, which is why I couldn't arrange an exhibition on the spot, but by the end of this afternoon I'm sure the deal will be set.' He turned, smiling at Serena. 'You did bring the paintings back from England, didn't you?'

White, she nodded, unable to look up for fear she would encounter Nick's blue gaze.

'Good girl!' said Phil, and put his hand over hers, smiling, as though they were alone and he could be as familiar as he always was; but of course they weren't alone, and Nick saw that familiarity, his eyes lifting to Serena's face with an expression that made her hair stand on end.

The waiter was pouring their champagne. Chatter was going on all around them. Phil was still talking about art, galleries, exhibitions…

'Yes, of course you must come back to the apartment with us,' Nick said sardonically as their *hors-d'oeuvres* were served. 'And we must all look at my wife's paintings.'

After lunch, which Serena had barely even picked at, they drove back in Nick's long black Cadillac limousine to Fifth Avenue. The chauffeur was cool, silent, efficient, gliding through the heavy New York traffic with great skill.

'So—' Nick strode into the apartment, his face set like stone '—where are your paintings, my love?'

'In my wardrobe,' she said with a deep sense of growing alarm.

He looked at her. 'Go and get them.'

Serena swallowed, looking at Phil accusingly through her lashes. He frowned at her, as he had done throughout this very uncomfortable meeting, and she wondered if he was stupid. Couldn't he sense the tension between herself and her husband?

Serena opened her wardrobe and took out the paintings, all fifteen of them, unframed and unseen by anyone but Serena until now.

Clutching them with shaking fingers, she felt a deep resentment that this had happened. They were her life. Her identity. And she had nurtured them with possessive care. Would this moment of revelation smash them forever, and her growing sense of identity with them?

Nick suddenly knocked at the door and came in, halting in the doorway, his face a cool mask.

Their eyes clashed across the bedroom floor. Resentment shimmered like green fire in Serena's eyes. She felt a sudden new wave of hatred for him, and it showed.

'I came to see if you needed a hand,' Nick said coolly.

She clutched her paintings, unable to reply for fear she might break down and cry. He was looking at her oddly, studying the paintings as she clutched them to her breasts.

'I'd also like to see them first,' he said flatly. 'Would you mind?'

She stared, taken aback, then coloured, shaking her head. 'Of course not.'

Nick walked coolly towards her, taking them as she stepped away from him. He laid them all out, propped against the wardrobe. He stepped back, hands thrust deep in black trouser-pockets, and surveyed them with a hard expression.

Serena trembled inside with nerves. What did she care what Nick thought of her work? He was just her owner, the man who had bought her from her parents for the price of Flaxton Manor! Yet suddenly his eyes on those paintings were more important to her than all the exhibitions in the world...

He stared at the swirls of barbaric colour, the fire leaping from the canvases, the bright flashes and flares of light against darkness, the passionate use of oils, thickly applied with knife and brush.

'You're a primitive!' he said at once, and shot her a thoughtful look.

Her lashes flickered and she felt a smile curve her mouth. 'Oh...I know...someone told me that before...'

Nick's mouth tightened. 'Greyson?'

She nodded, watching him.

He looked back at the paintings, then a smile touched his mouth and he murmured, 'That one is fantastic...!'

She frowned. 'Which...?'

He pointed to the gypsy dancer in red, swirling in vivid slashes of colour against a blazing camp-fire. 'It looks like you...'

Serena laughed softly, flushing and lowering her lashes.

'Don't be shy,' he said under his breath, and suddenly his strong hands were sliding to her waist as he turned, and before she could look up he was pulling her against his hard body, saying thickly, 'You're very talented, Serena. I had no idea...'

Heart thudding at his touch, she tried to pull away. 'Phil will be late for work if we don't hurry...'

'Damn Phil!' he said tightly, anger creeping into his blue eyes, but he released her and collected the paintings up, his mouth hard as he picked them up and carried them into the living-room.

Later, they were spread out on the table and Phil was enthusing over the plans for an exhibition. Serena had painted thirty paintings in the last six months— or, rather, completed thirty. She worked in a whirlwind of chaos, blasting raw images on to the canvases very quickly, then recovering with exhilarated exhaustion and a sense of achievement.

'A shame you didn't finish the others.' Phil sighed, disappointed. 'You must try to complete them in future, or you'll waste time and money.'

She gave a wry smile. 'I get interrupted, Phil. And once I've been interrupted, my mind is dislodged. I lose the painting.'

'You lose the motivational force,' Nick said flatly, watching her with narrowed eyes.

Serena nodded slowly, meeting his blue gaze. He looked so gorgeous, leaning on the table, his black jacket off, his black waistcoat tight and emphasising the lean power of his torso, his silk tie loosened, shirt undone at the neck to expose his strong, tanned throat.

Beside him, Phil looked young and thin and rather effeminate suddenly. Serena caught herself short with a fast-beating heart. Nick's potent masculinity had always made her feel threatened—hadn't it?

'Well—' Phil straightened suddenly, glancing at his watch '—I have to get back to the gallery. I've got a client interested in selling me a Picasso.'

'How much for?' Nick asked at once, interested.

'I'm not at liberty to say,' Phil demurred, smiling. 'But I shall draw up the contract for you, Lady Serena, and—'

'Would you like me to handle the legalities for you, darling?' Nick put in coolly, shooting her a narrow-eyed look.

Her heart skipped a beat at that look. 'Thank you,' she heard herself say huskily, 'that would be very kind of you.'

His mouth curved in a hard smile and he straightened, thrusting his hands into the pockets of his black trousers, towering a good six inches over Phil, his authority a potent force.

'We'll hear from you shortly, then?' he drawled.

'Of course.' Phil nodded. 'I'll call round tonight, in fact, if that's still convenient...?'

'Tonight!' Nick's dark brows met sharply and his head swung to stare at Serena.

'Well, yes...' Phil said, looking from one to the other. 'I'd arranged to take Lady Serena to the opera. Didn't she tell you?'

'No,' Nick said under his breath, a dangerous note to his voice as his eyes narrowed on her face. 'She did not.'

CHAPTER FOUR

SERENA quavered inwardly as she saw Phil to the door. Nick hadn't taken it well at all. Obviously, he didn't like the thought of his wife going to the opera with another man. But Phil wasn't another man—he was just a friend of hers.

'Are you sure it'll be all right?' Phil whispered, *sotto voce*, at the door. 'He didn't seem pleased to me.'

Serena lifted gold brows, saying softly, 'I see him so rarely. I can't believe he'll make any real objections. After all, I am entitled to my own life.'

Phil looked down into her green eyes with a smile. 'Yes...you're entitled to more than that, Serena.' Without warning he bent his head and kissed her mouth, then drew back. 'See you at seven-thirty! Outside the Met...'

Serena stared, astonished by that kiss. Phil had become close to her over the last month. He had often kissed her hand, her cheek—but never her mouth.

Closing the door, she went back into the living-room to find Nick waiting for her like a dark, brooding presence. Her pulses skipped at the sight of him, his black head bent, eyes narrowed, hands thrust in black trouser-pockets.

'Would you like some coffee?' she asked carefully,

anxious for the opportunity to escape from the prospect of discussing sex again. It had always been a secret fear. She had known he would one day blast back into her life and demand sex.

'No,' Nick said, looking at her with those steely eyes. 'I don't want some coffee. I want to know exactly what you think you're playing at with Greyson.'

She leapt on to the new subject with overwhelming relief. 'Well, I thought that was obvious. He's arranging an exhibition for—'

'I'm not talking about your business relationship,' Nick clipped out harshly.

'We have no other relationship.' Serena stiffened at the implication in his words. 'Obviously, he's a friend of mine, but there's no more to it than that.'

'Really?' he drawled with cynical mockery. 'You may frequent the Met with business friends of the opposite sex, but I can assure you I don't!'

Her green eyes flashed. 'Well, I wouldn't know about that, would I, Nick? Your entire life has always been a mystery to me. For all I know, you take your business friends to bed. Presumably that's why you're making such nasty remarks about Phil and me.' Turning on her heel, she stormed into the kitchen.

He followed her at a long stride, his eyes angry. 'I've been frank with you about my life from day one. I work, I travel, I make money and I take beautiful women to bed.'

'Charming!' she snapped, jealous fire in her eyes. 'You talk like a machete—did you know that?'

'Only when you bug me,' he said flatly, standing in the doorway. 'And who the hell are you to accuse me

of keeping my life a mystery? I come back out of the
blue and find you're hiding secrets in every damned
cupboard.'

'Secrets!' She shook her head. 'Really, Nick. I'm
just trying to live my own life. A life you've never
been a part of.'

'Well, I'm part of it now,' he said with an arrogant
lift of his brows. 'So start spilling the beans. One: who
exactly is this Greyson guy to you? Two: when did
you turn into Van Gogh? Three: how many other little
businessman friends are you hiding behind my back?'

She gave an angry laugh. 'Have you ever heard the
phrase, mind your own business?'

'You insolent little bitch!' he bit out under his
breath, and strode towards her.

'I'm sorry!' she whispered, backing, hands up in
self-defence.

He stopped just in front of her, bristling with aggression. Serena was trembling as she stared up at him,
her heart banging against her breastbone.

'It is my business, Serena,' Nick said. 'Everything
you do is my business. So we'll take it from the beginning, shall we? What exactly has been going on in
your life over the last three years?'

She drew an unsteady breath. 'Nothing much. I...I
spent the first two years just drifting, really.'

'Be more specific,' he said flatly.

'Well, that's the funny thing about drifting,' she said
sarcastically. 'It's a most unspecific occupation.'

'Don't be clever. Just stick to the story.'

'All right,' she snapped. 'The story—I drifted
around in an empty marriage and an empty life.' She

studied him with resentment. 'What was I supposed to do? You destroyed my life, Nick. You married me for my title, uprooted me from my house, and set me down in a strange world with no friends, no purpose and nothing whatever to do.'

The blue eyes narrowed. 'You make it sound as though I deliberately isolated you, but that isn't the case. You isolated yourself.'

'Rubbish!'

'It was your life,' he said flatly. 'Your responsibility. If you chose to do nothing but drift about from New York to Hong Kong, attending cocktail parties and feeling bored, that's your problem.'

Her eyes burned with anger. 'I didn't know what else to do. I had no friends of my own and no job to do.'

'That's marriage for you,' he said coolly. 'Most women find themselves in a similar situation. What makes you so different?'

'Most women have their husbands,' she said bitterly.

'And most wives go to bed with them,' he bit out.

'Only when they've married for love. You don't even like me, Nick. You never contacted me, you never sent me a postcard.' Her eyes blazed fiercely green. 'You never even bothered to show up except at Christmas.'

'Why should I?' he said flatly. 'When I spend time with a woman I expect her to be beautiful, exciting and accommodating. Not someone who just stares at me in hostile silence, boiling over with resentment.'

'If I boiled over with resentment it was because I was unhappy!'

'What did you expect me to do? Wave a magic wand and send you to the ball?' His mouth hardened. 'That only happens in fairy-stories. In real life you build your own coach, make your own dress, and haul your own cookies to the ball.'

'Well, it took me a long time to decide which ball I wanted to go to,' she said furiously. 'How does that grab you?'

He stared at her for a second, then started to laugh, blue eyes moving with lazy amusement over her angry face. 'Since when did you start talking like me?'

She lifted her red head with proud hauteur. 'Since I started living in your world, Nick.'

'Good reply,' he drawled, eyes narrowing. 'But hardly accurate. You live in your own world now, Serena, and I want to know exactly what that world is.'

'Well, unless you're deaf,' she said coolly, 'you already know, because Phil told you practically everything over lunch.'

'And you didn't like that, did you?' he challenged with an arch of black brows. 'I could see you desperately trying to shut him up. Not very discreet, is he? Unless he was deliberately trying to cause trouble...'

'Don't be ridiculous,' she said flatly. 'Besides—why shouldn't I want you to know that I'm now an artist?'

'You tell me.'

She moistened her lips, darting her gaze from him. There was a little silence. The kitchen was filled with sunlight, and her back was against the wall.

'When did you start painting?' Nick asked point-blank.

She gave an irritable sigh. 'Oh, I forget.'

'No, you don't,' he drawled, laughing under his breath. 'I'll bet you remember the day, the hour, the minute. So come on—out with it. When did the muse strike you?'

Her lips tightened. She folded her arms, resenting him.

'Hell!' Nick said tightly, watching her. 'It's like trying to get blood out of the proverbial stone.' His hand touched her chin, forcing her to look at him as he said with hard mockery, 'You're not leaving this room until you tell me what I want to know.'

'You can't pry my head open,' she said angrily, glaring at him.

'No, but I can cut your ear off and make you paint a self-portrait,' he drawled.

She smiled against her will. Her green eyes flashed to his face, considering him for a moment. He was obviously determined. However much she resented him for prying into her life like this, she could see he wasn't going to give up until he had extracted at least enough information to satisfy him—for the moment.

'All right,' she said slowly, prickling with resentment. 'I started painting in September. The gypsy was my first painting. I kept it hidden, but I added to it. Just couldn't stop painting. By Christmas, I had about fifteen canvases. I decided I might be able to sell them, so I started haunting galleries.'

'And met Greyson,' he said, eyes narrowing. 'Are there any others like him?'

'What do you mean—others like him?'

'Men who want to take you out for little business chats,' he drawled unpleasantly.

Her face flamed. 'No, there are not. Phil is setting up an exhibition for me—nothing more. Besides—why should you be remotely interested in all this? You're going to disappear out of my life again—don't tell me you're not. You always do.'

'Not this time, Serena,' he said softly, and slid his hand down to caress her naked throat, invoking shivers. 'I'm back to close this deal—remember?'

Bitterness flashed in her eyes. 'By making me go to bed with you until I give you your precious heir? Wonderful! I can hardly wait!'

'Glad to hear it,' he drawled softly. 'Because I've come back into your life with one goal in mind—the bedroom door. It's time I kicked it open, Serena. You can fight all you want, but I'm the strongest and, as we all know—the strongest always wins.'

She shuddered convulsively, staring. 'You don't need me...you have mistresses...plenty of willing women, you said.'

'You're right. I don't need you. But I do need children.'

'I'm not ready...'

'Yes, you are.'

She gave a fragile laugh, green eyes stricken. 'From the way you're talking, I suppose I'll have to be. You're obviously serious about forcing children on me.'

'Forcing?' he asked, ruthless mouth hardening. 'Don't you want them?'

'Yes,' she said without thinking, her voice oddly husky. 'I want them very much.' It didn't occur to her to question that statement or where it had come from. 'But not from you, Nick. I'd rather die than bring a son of yours into the world.'

His teeth met. 'Don't ever say that to me again, you little—'

'Why not?' she demanded fiercely. 'It's how I feel. You ruined my life once, and now that I've rebuilt it you're going to smash it all to pieces! I feel powerless to stop you!' Her mouth shook. 'And I hate feeling that way!'

His blue eyes gleamed with malice. 'Poor little helpless aristocrat!'

Rage shot through her. Her hand moved to slap his hard, mocking face and he laughed at her, catching her wrist in strong fingers, amused by her puny struggles.

'Well, well, well!' he drawled, laughing. 'The future Countess of Archallagen doing something most dishonourable.'

'You're dishonourable,' she spat, struggling furiously. 'You!'

'Am I, Serena?' he bit out, blue eyes like steel. 'I never welshed on a deal in my life.'

She fell silent, flushing hotly, staring at him through her lashes. What could she do or say? He was right. But at the same time so wrong, so horribly wrong.

Nick released her suddenly, his mouth hard. 'Make that coffee. I'll be in the living-room.'

Mutinously, she rubbed her wrist, staring after him as he strode out of the kitchen. The truth was coming out between them now. And it was vile. This was the reality of their marriage. Nick had bought her for her title and he wanted an heir to one day sit in the House of Lords. That was all there was to it.

Nick was on the phone when she went into the living-room. Carrying his coffee to his side, she placed it on the telephone table, her eyes enquiring.

He was sitting like a man in the grip of sexual attraction, his chest thrown out, one arm along the back of the couch. He smiled, his voice lazily charming, and occasionally ran a hand through his dark hair.

A woman, she thought, tensing. He's talking to a woman. Jealousy hit her like a knife. Trembling, she moved to an armchair and sank down in it, hating him, hating herself. Why should she feel jealousy? She hated Nick, wanted nothing more than for him to turn to other women, keep all his mistresses, make love to them instead of her...

Yet the thought of his making love to another woman was suddenly like bitter poison to her...

'Seven-thirty, then?' he was drawling into the telephone, a sardonic smile on his hard mouth. 'Right... OK...bye!' He replaced the receiver and looked at her with a glitter of satisfaction in his eyes.

'Going out tonight?' she asked tightly, hating him.

'Mmm,' he murmured. 'With Monique.'

Her hand shook as she raised her coffee-cup to her mouth and drank. When she had a hold on herself again, she said, 'So where are you going with Monique?'

'The opera,' he said softly, and his blue eyes glinted with sardonic mockery as he watched the slow flush rise up her face.

'You can't be serious!' she said rawly, putting her cup down.

'Why not?' he drawled, smiling. 'After all—I don't want the whole of New York to realise the extent of our open marriage.'

'Open…!'

'That is what you've told Greyson, isn't it?' he cut in harshly, arching dark brows.

Her eyes flashed. 'I haven't told Phil anything at all!'

'Then why is he happy to make blatant advances to my wife in front of me?' he bit out, his mouth hardening.

'What?' Serena stared at him, her lips parting. 'Phil…make advances to me…?'

He gave a harsh laugh. 'He invited you on a date right in front of me!' The blue eyes blazed with hard anger. 'What did you tell him, Serena? That I didn't give a damn what you did in your private life? That I had plenty of mistresses and wouldn't bat an eyelid if you had an affair yourself?'

She sucked in her breath. 'Just because you live in that kind of world, it doesn't mean everybody does!' she burst out hoarsely. 'Phil would never dream of—'

'Oh, he'd dream it all right!' Nick bit out, getting to his feet, his eyes fierce. 'In fact, he spent the whole four hours he was here dreaming of it! Right under my nose!' He strode towards her, his mouth shaking suddenly as he towered over her, bristling with aggression. 'The impertinent little bastard! I had to practically bite my knuckles to stop myself punching his face through the back of his—'

'No!' Serena stood up too, green eyes flaring as she faced him. 'Phil is a friend! Nothing more! He's never at any time—'

'The hell he hasn't,' Nick bit out thickly. 'I saw the way he was looking at you. He couldn't take his damned eyes off you. And he kept touching you. Endless intimate little gestures.'

'You're imagining it!' she said fiercely. 'It's that filthy mind of yours, Nick. It ties you up in knots because it's the way you think, and you imagine every other man thinks the same way.'

'They do when they look at you!' he said hoarsely, dark colour invading his face as his breathing grew ragged and the atmosphere tilted to that dark sexual landscape which terrified her so much as she stared up at him, her heart thudding painfully in her chest.

'They don't think like that...' she whispered, and it hurt to breathe.

'My God,' he said tightly, reaching for her, 'do you still have no idea what you do to me, Serena? To all men? You're the most rampantly sexual creature I've ever encountered in my life.'

She sucked in her breath, trying to back away, found herself trapped against the chair and almost overbalanced, giving a little cry, her hands shooting to his broad shoulders.

'You were like mortal sin when I first saw you,' Nick said thickly, strong hands moving like fire over her slender shoulders as he stared down at her. 'I can remember looking up at that window and feeling the hair on my scalp stand on end with—'

'Don't!' she whispered, her face burning.

'That unbelievably sexy body,' he said under his breath, 'in that demure lace dress. The combination sent me up in flames, Serena. And those green eyes…my God, you're a born seductress.'

'I am not!'

He stared at her, his hands moving through her hair. 'You look at me like a siren, with all that red hair falling over one eye, and your beautiful mouth parted…' His voice roughened. 'And you wonder why I want to take you to bed!'

'To get an heir,' she breathed hoarsely, hands shaking on his shoulders. 'That's all it is!'

'Do you seriously think I'd have married you if you were short, fat and ugly?'

'That only makes you all the more despicable!'

His mouth hardened. 'I don't give a damn if you find me despicable. I married you for my own purposes, and if you don't start to co-operate and fulfil them, Serena, I'll have to take a very tough line with you.'

'What are you saying? That you'll force me?' she asked bitterly.

'I won't need to,' he said under his breath. 'Your response to me since I returned has been more than encouraging. I think the truth is that you want me as much as I want you. You have since you first saw me.'

'No!' The hot denial sprang from her lips.

'Oh, yes,' he said softly, and ran one long finger down her white throat, invoking shivers, making her heart thud treacherously fast. 'All I need to do is kiss you till your head spins. Sooner or later, you'll spin into bed with me, and then I'll really give you something to spin about.'

'Oh, God...' she whispered in sick excitement, and pushed at his shoulders, her stomach clenching as she struggled to get away from him, her breathing intolerably fast.

'Kiss me!' Nick said thickly, and swept her into his powerful arms, his mouth closing over hers, eliciting a hoarse moan of pleasure from her, and her mouth was parting helplessly beneath his, her hands clinging to his strong neck as she pressed her slender body against the hard masculinity of his and shook with excitement.

Treacherous...her body was the traitor...she couldn't fight the tidal-waves of sensual desire that were flooding her, and as the kiss deepened she was moaning, her fingers pushing restlessly into his dark hair.

Suddenly, fear rose in her, anger and hatred too, and she gave a hoarse cry of panic, pushing away from him. He was too startled to stop her.

Breaking away from him, she ran across the room to her bedroom.

'Come back here!' Nick followed her at a hellish pace, voice thick with rage and desire. 'I haven't finished with you yet.'

Slamming the door in his face, she locked it, her fingers shaking, and backed away from the closed door in fear and excitement as he rattled the handle violently.

'It just gets better, Serena,' he said thickly through the door. 'More of the same, and the excitement you just felt can spiral right up to ecstasy…Serena…open the damned door.'

'Go away!' she said furiously. 'Just go away and leave me alone!'

'So you can start an affair with Greyson?' he bit out. 'Like hell I will!' He rattled the door-handle again angrily. 'You can stay in there and hide for as long as you like, Serena. But sooner or later you're going to have to come to terms with my presence in your life. As your husband, Serena.' He slammed the door with one hand. 'Your husband!'

'I can hardly forget that, can I?' she shouted, suddenly overflowing with rage as she stared at that locked door. 'You've made it more than clear that you're back to get what you wanted from me in the first place!'

'That's right,' his voice said tightly. 'And by the time you give it to me it's going to be willingly. I'm your husband—and I will be your lover!'

'You'll have to force me!' she shouted at the closed door. 'I won't be able to stop you, but I will be able to hate you for it!'

'Hate me as much as you want,' he drawled tightly. 'I never wanted your love or your affection or your good opinion. I want one thing and one thing only: and, believe me, Serena, I *will* get it.'

His footsteps receded, his bedroom door slammed, and Serena stood there with his threats ringing in her ears, and her mouth bruised from the devastating passion of his kisses.

How she hated him for doing this. She had known instinctively that he was lying about the jet's breaking down. From the minute she'd woken to find him in her bed she had felt the shock waves of sexual desire, and now they were threatening to destroy her life.

And he was so clever. So careful to keep it all under wraps until he had got a deep niche carved both in her and in their apartment. Once he was sure the time was right for this, he showed his hand.

Damn him. He would drive her crazy with his ruthless manipulation. He had been here for forty-eight hours and she was reeling like a bumper car from the impact.

If he had been direct with her, honest with her, she could have dealt with it. But he hadn't. He had told lie after lie, and, every now and then, out came the truth in his steely voice as he probed for the answers to questions only he knew about.

He wasn't going to stop, either. He really was determined to make her have children with him, and although she wanted children she didn't want to go to bed with Nick Colterne.

He wants to confuse me, she realised angrily. He wants to turn me upside-down by using those clever tactics of his. And he'll get what he wants if I'm not careful, she realised with a thudding heart—he'll dodge through every defence I've got, manipulating and lying until we're face to face in bed and I've got no escape.

Serena took a very long bath, emerging with wet hair and a softly scented body. As she blow-dried her long red-gold hair into its usual style she suddenly noticed her reflection.

Rampantly sexual, Nick had said...she frowned,

studying herself, her full mouth in its customary pout, her slanting green eyes curiously deep and quite powerful in their fathomless intensity.

Dismissing her thoughts as though they were dangerous, she began to dress. Frowning in front of her expensive wardrobe, she knew she must select a dress that would not bring further accusations from Nick.

She chose a dove-grey chiffon and silk dress. It was high-necked, a slim-fitting silk shift covered in pearl-grey chiffon, the sleeves demure and transparent. Against her long red-gold hair and vivid green eyes, it looked almost invisible; but very elegant and ladylike.

Slipping her feet into grey high heels, she caught sight of her reflection and suddenly remembered how she had looked when Nick first saw her, in that little lace dress, so ill-fitting and childlike, straining against her full breasts and hips...

An air of sophistication had crept over her in the three years of their marriage. Serena straightened, staring at herself, realising how unrecognisable she was now from that gauche, gawky teenager.

When she went into the living-room at seven it was empty. Nick had gone. Her heart sank as she looked at his open bedroom door. He had left without even saying goodbye.

Unaccountably, pain shot through her. Letting herself out of the apartment, she went down in the air-conditioned lift, her green eyes brooding and bitter. Nick patently could not wait to see Monique...

'Evening, Lady Serena!' the doorman drawled as

she went out into the hot, brightly lit Manhattan street. 'Enjoying the heat wave?'

'It's wonderful!' she said with a smile. 'I do love to see New York relax. Everyone's wearing such pretty clothes…'

The door man laughed. 'Your accent always gets me!' He turned, the sun lilting on the gold braid of his red cap. 'You want a cab?'

'Please.' She pushed a swath of red-gold hair back. 'To the Met.' The thought of bumping into Nick there with his mistress was now a source of horror to her. What would she say to Phil? How could she possibly explain the fact that she and her husband were blatantly displaying their mutual indifference to the world?

The Met was ravishing in the evening sunlight. Serena stepped from the cab on to the hot pavement, walked with her usual quick stride to the fountains, green eyes flashing around for a sign of Phil.

In the dove-grey chiffon dress her slender curves caused a riot of male attention, her quick stride making her sway, hips moving with unconscious sexuality.

Suddenly, she saw him and caught her breath with a shock. He stood a few feet away. Nick lounged beside him, indolent and handsome in a black evening suit, the impeccable cut of that expensive material enhancing the air of power and wealth he carried with him like an invisible cloak.

'Lady Serena!' Phil waved and smiled. 'Over here!'

Serena's eyes raced to Nick's hard face as he studied her coolly, a gleam of mockery in his blue eyes, a sardonic twist to his mouth. Monique Dupré, of course, stood at his side, radiating thin, expensive glamour.

'I managed to exchange our seats for a box,' Nick drawled sardonically as Serena approached with a furious face. 'Isn't that swell?'

'We'll all be sitting together,' Phil said, brushing his blond hair back with one elegant, smooth hand. 'And we'll get a much better view of the stage.'

'I doubt that,' Serena said tightly, heart thudding with rage. 'Not with four of us in the box!'

'This is the best box in the house, darling,' Nick said softly, watching her through his hooded eyelids. 'And I know you love the best of everything.'

Serena gave him a bitter smile, and flicked her gaze at last to the white-skinned, red-lipped face of Monique Dupré, standing beside him, tall and willowy and utterly magnificent in clinging black silk. The woman was pencil-thin and looked like a fashion photograph.

Jealousy coiled in the pit of her stomach like fire but she was forced to smile at the older, more sophisticated woman. 'Hello, Monique. How are you?'

'Oh,' Monique drawled with a twist of glossy red lips, 'surviving. The heat wave is playing havoc with my perm, though!'

Serena was coolly polite, nodding. 'It's been a mad summer.'

'Shall we go in?' Nick murmured, unsmiling, and they all moved away together, crossing that elegant courtyard towards the hallowed portals of Manhattan's most civilised marble palace.

The deep-rooted feelings of familiarity in Serena

rose at once as she entered the chandeliered foyer. Those high ceilings, the elegant patrons, the strong air of hushed sophistication all combined to bring back memories of her childhood, attending Covent Garden with her parents, garden parties at Buck House, meeting her father for tea at the House of Lords…she had always preferred those moments of her life with them. The glamour and excitement had been brief flashes of colour in her otherwise quiet life at Flaxton Manor. Her parents had known that, too, but they had been so old, and they had not quite known what to do with the red-haired firecracker who was their daughter.

Nick led the way into the box. 'Serena?' he drawled, indicating the red velvet chair on his right.

Shooting him an angry glance, she moved forward and took her place beside him. Down below, people in the audience looked up, recognising them. No doubt Nick only wanted her to sit with him to ensure no ugly rumours started, and suddenly Serena agreed with him: it had never before entered her head that people might think they had an open marriage.

'I just love this place,' Phil drawled, sitting on Serena's right. 'It's so damned awe-inspiring!'

Serena gave him a surprised look. 'You don't feel ill-at-ease, do you, Phil?'

He ran a hand through his blond hair. 'A little. I'm from the Bronx, remember, and we don't get too many chandeliers down there!'

'I've never been to the Bronx,' Serena said, smiling. 'When did you move to New York?'

'When I was nineteen,' he said with a grin. 'Been here ever since, making money and sharpening up my artistic inclinations.' He gestured to the auditorium. 'Like visiting the Met, to see and be seen...a lot of deals are made in the interval, important contacts, lunches arranged.' His blond brows lifted. 'It's where the top people meet.'

'They tend to come here,' Nick said coolly beside Serena, 'to watch the opera, not the audience.'

'Well, sure,' Phil drawled. 'But there's no harm in making the most of your opportunities, is there?'

'No,' Nick said flatly, watching him through narrowed eyes, 'and I had you pegged as an opportunist from the very beginning.'

There was an uncomfortable little silence. Phil tensed slightly, his face suddenly guarded as he met Nick Colterne's shrewd blue gaze and sensed the more powerful, more deadly, more ruthless shark suddenly appearing before him.

'Are you,' Nick asked softly, a thread of steel in his voice, 'an opportunist, Greyson?'

Phil cleared his throat. 'Sir, I'm just trying to make an honest buck.'

'Be sure it is honest,' Nick enunciated coolly, 'or you'll find my teeth in your jugular.'

Serena caught her breath. The lights went down. The tension in the box was suddenly intolerable. In the darkness, Phil pursed his lips in a silent whistle.

Monique moved her chair closer to Nick, and Serena saw her slide a long red-taloned hand over his hard thigh. Rage blinded her suddenly. The overture was playing, the curtain going up, and the brightly lit stage filled with colourful drama as the opera began, but Serena barely saw it; all she could see was that red-

taloned hand sliding possessively over Nick's hard
thigh, and she began to tremble with the deep sense
of injustice and jealousy she felt.

The horror of her marriage was suddenly laid bare
before her, and she almost choked on the pain she felt
clutching her throat, hot tears stinging her eyes as the
opera went on and on.

La Bohème was one of her favourites, but she barely
saw it, although the rich vein of pain in Puccini's music reached her soul, as it always did, and sent shivers
through her. She had always felt deeply moved by
Puccini, and as she sat beside her ruthless husband she
understood why, because the pain she felt was directly
echoed by the soaring emotion of the soprano on stage.

The interval was a nightmare as they drank together
in the bar, she and her husband and their respective
partners. Nick watched Monique's red mouth with a
sardonic smile as she talked to him, flirting openly,
and Serena was glad to get back to their box so she
wouldn't have to watch any more.

When the opera was over they streamed out into the
night along with the glittering array of Manhattan's
élite.

'I'm taking Monique home in the limousine,' Nick
drawled, hands thrust in the pockets of his black evening suit. 'You don't mind, do you, darling? I'm sure
you have…similar plans yourself.'

Serena blanched, appalled by his deliberate humiliation of her in front of Phil, and whispered through
white lips, 'Why should I mind what you do with your
mistress?' Then she turned on her heel and walked

angrily away from them all, her eyes burning with a red mist.

'Wait!' Phil caught up with her, blond hair flying in the warm night breeze. 'Don't let the bastard get to you!' He caught her arm, his dark eyes concerned. 'He's just not worth it!'

'Oh, God, I can't go on like this much longer!' she said fiercely, staring bitterly across the floodlit court-yard as Nick strode with Monique, his hand at the small of her back, towards the waiting limousine. 'I just can't live with this marriage any more!'

'Don't talk here!' Phil said quickly, looking around as people passed them, staring openly. 'Come on... let's get you home and you can tell me all about it there!' He strode with her to the road, calling for a taxi, and Serena went numbly, aware that her marriage had finally hit rock-bottom.

CHAPTER FIVE

HE HAD been so blatant. So amused by the humiliation he had inflicted on her. And Serena couldn't understand the jealous pain clawing at her, the sense of total dark chaos she felt. After years of polite indifference to each other, their marriage was cracking wide open and it felt like Nick's fist through the pane of glass she had sheltered behind. The glass was shattered now, pieces everywhere, and Serena was a woman covered in broken glass, staring into her husband's deadly face.

She let herself into the luxurious apartment, her face white and strained. Throwing her keys on the hall table, Serena walked into the living-room, flicking on the lights, and looked at it with new eyes.

'How long has it been like this?' Phil asked huskily behind her, and she turned, staring at him, because she had forgotten he was there.

'I...' She put a hand to her temple. 'I don't know. Forever, I suppose. The hatred must have been there all the time. I just didn't know it...didn't want to know it...'

'You've always lived separate lives?' he questioned, dark eyes probing hers. 'Separate... personal lives?'

Her mouth twisted bitterly. 'If you're asking what I

think you're asking, you can forget it! I would no more take a lover or even consider a relationship with—'

'Serena, I must ask,' he said roughly, and put his hands on her slim shoulders, startling her. 'It was obvious when I first saw you that you were lonely, bored, unloved. I never realised the extent of it, though, until tonight.'

'Don't, Phil...' she pleaded, wincing. 'I didn't realise it myself. I...I suppose I've just been forced to face it, and I really don't like what I see.'

Phil studied her with dark eyes. 'He's never loved you?'

'Never.' Bitterly, she shook her red-gold head, moving away from him across the living-room towards the windows, those wide windows that looked across New York, and the Chrysler building looked achingly beautiful tonight against the razzle-dazzle skyline.

'Why did you marry him?' Phil asked, watching her.

Stiffening, she said bleakly, 'Does it matter why?' A loyalty to Nick that she could not fight any more than she could understand flared up inside her, and she knew that she would never tell Phil the truth of her reasons for marrying. 'I did, that's all, and this is the result.' She gave a husky laugh, eyes shimmering with tears. 'I always knew Nick didn't love me. It just never occurred to me that I would ever find that situation intolerable.'

'You could divorce him.' Phil swept up beside her suddenly, watching her acutely, his eyes narrowed.

'No,' she said at once. 'Out of the question.' Her deep-rooted sense of honour made divorce impossible. So did her dislike of scandal. If she and Nick ever went through the divorce courts, his mistresses would be plastered all over the front pages, and Serena could not have faced that, any more than she could have done it to Nick.

Nick, for all that he was a ruthless bastard, was also from a charming and dignified family. A family with a spotless reputation. Pillars of Bostonian society, and proud of their successful son, if a little uneasy with him.

During their married life, Serena had only met his parents half a dozen times. They were a quiet couple, elegant and polite, completely overshadowed by their powerful son. They stayed in their world; Nick stayed in his.

But Serena knew he loved his family deeply, and it would be a bitter blow if a divorce scandal erupted around him, shaming him in front of them and their Boston friends.

It was a further twist of the knife to know that divorce was impossible because of her powerful and inexplicable loyalty to Nick Colterne. How she hated him...

'I couldn't divorce Nick,' she heard her raw voice say with angry acceptance. 'Not ever.'

'But that's madness, Serena!' Phil turned her to face him. 'He just humiliated you deliberately in front of his mistress!'

'I can't divorce him, don't ask again!' she whispered, and wrenched herself away from him, struggling to deal with the bitter pain his words invoked. 'Phil, you've got to understand. Nick and I—we have an understanding. Regardless of the rights and wrongs,

I agreed to this marriage, and I'll have to live with it.' Her lips were suddenly bloodless as she remembered Nick's words this morning and found herself repeating them. 'I'll have to find some way to come to terms with it...'

'When you say that you and Nick have an "understanding",' Phil said slowly, watching her, 'do you mean this was a marriage of convenience?'

Serena gave a harsh sigh and looked away. 'I can't discuss it...'

'OK.' Phil was thinking on his feet. 'You can't discuss it, but that doesn't stop me guessing. And my guess is that money is at the bottom of this.'

Serena looked away jerkily, her face white.

'It is money, isn't it?' Phil raised blond brows. 'You needed his money and he fancied you, so you got married.'

She winced, unable to speak. It sounded so vile...

'Presumably you still need his money,' Phil said slowly. 'But that's the beauty of all this. Don't you see? Divorce is a multi-million-dollar business.' He moved closer, excitement in his dark eyes. 'Serena, you could take that bastard to the cleaners and walk away with half his fortune!'

'I'm going to pretend I didn't hear you say that, Phil.' Her voice was rough with horror. 'It's the most appalling suggestion anyone has ever made to me.'

'More appalling than marrying a man you can't stand for his money?' Phil bit back, flushing darkly.

Serena whitened, unable to reply.

'It's true, isn't it?' Phil pressed his advantage home ruthlessly. 'You married him for his money, but you

can't stand the sight of him. And I don't blame you.
Not after tonight. The way he spoke to me was bad
enough, but the way he treated you was totally unacceptable.'

He was right and she had no clever reply, no way
of explaining how deep her pain went, how loyal she
felt to Nick, how angry she was at the thought of anyone wanting to drag him through the legal mud in front
of his family.

'You're right,' she said bitterly. 'Nick's behaviour
was unacceptable tonight. But I can't do it to him, Phil.
I just can't contemplate—hurting him like that.'

'Hurting him!' Phil took her shoulders, his dark eyes
blazing. 'What about you?'

'I've got my work,' she said with a tight smile. 'I'm
quite happy, just painting and seeing friends, going to
art exhibitions…I don't need anything else from life,
Phil! Certainly not the horror divorce would bring!'

'You need love!' Phil said fiercely. 'You're a beautiful, vibrant woman and you need a man who can
make love to you, give love to you, take love from
you!'

She gave a rough laugh, tears in her eyes. 'So all
the magazines tell me!'

'Don't joke about it, Serena!' Phil said hoarsely, and
suddenly he was staring at her full mouth in a way
that made her feel very uneasy indeed. 'Not with
me…not after all this time…'

Her eyes widened and she caught her breath.
'Phil—'

'My darling, I've been so patient!' he said tensely,
and his hands were tightening on her slim shoulders.

'I could see you were completely unaware of your own frustration. I could see you were lonely and unloved, and I could see that cold diamond on your finger, next to the wedding band, and no husband in sight...'

'Phil, I can't believe you're saying any of this.' She was trying carefully to extricate herself from him, her eyes alarmed as she suddenly sensed danger. 'I've always been frank with you. My husband is a busy man and that's why we were never together—'

'That's what you said,' he cut in. 'But it wasn't what your eyes told me, or your body, or your special smiles.'

'My special smiles!' she echoed, horrified, staring at him.

'Serena, I've spent the last month trying to break through the dreamy barriers you throw up, and tonight's finally smashed them to pieces, hasn't it, my darling?'

'Phil—' she said in a warning voice.

'You're finally a real woman!' His dark eyes gleamed on her mouth. 'No dreams or illusions in your eyes. Just a woman in need of love, and I'm going to give it to you, Serena. I'm going to—'

'No!' she broke out fiercely, struggling, but it was too late, Phil was determined and believed everything he had said, and although she fought him he pulled her hard against him and his mouth closed over hers.

Squirming, Serena registered appalled distaste as his clammy mouth forced that unwanted kiss on her. It was a nightmare, his hands pushing her backwards towards the couch as she fought him.

'Don't deny yourself what you need!' Phil was saying thickly against her mouth as he manoeuvred her struggling body to the couch. 'What we both need! Serena, you're so lovely...!'

Crying out hoarsely for help that would not come, Serena felt herself falling backwards on to the couch. Phil joined her at once, pushing her down when she tried to sit up, his hands hard on her slim shoulders.

'You're passionate!' He was laughing, pressing his body down on hers to trap her there. 'I knew you would be! That sexy body...that red hair...those flashing eyes...!'

'Get your hands off me!' she choked out, but he just laughed and a second later his clammy mouth was back, his hands sliding up over her breasts to make her squirm in revulsion, hitting his shoulders, loathing him suddenly as their friendship was shattered by this gross sexual confrontation.

Suddenly, Phil wrenched himself away from her and flew across the floor.

Serena was baffled, staring as her mind groped to understand. Then she saw Nick towering over him, grabbing him by the scruff of his neck, lifting him to his feet.

'You heard the lady!' Nick said tightly. 'Get your filthy hands off her and keep them off!'

'Nick...!' Serena said rawly, sitting up, shaking. 'Don't hurt him...'

Nick laughed, flicking blue eyes over the younger, thinner man. 'Oh, I think he deserves to be hurt—don't you?'

'Not by you, Colterne!' Phil said with a quick, calculating glance at Serena. 'Not by a man who married an innocent young woman and ruined her life! You just wanted to—'

Nick punched him in the face. He watched Phil fly across the room and land on the floor against an armchair. Breathing thickly, he advanced on him, rage in his eyes.

He towered over him, bristling with menace and said in a thickly slurred voice, 'Don't you ever presume to talk about my marriage again!'

Phil stared up at him, a hand to his jaw. 'It's a little late to pretend you care about her, isn't it? You deserve to be dragged through the divorce courts and I'm going to stand beside Serena every step of the way!'

'Is that so?' Nick said under his breath, through his teeth.

'We've already discussed it!'

'I know,' Nick bit out, blue eyes deadly. 'You just asked her to take me to the cleaners.'

Phil's eyes widened, his face draining of all colour as he stared in silence at Nick, and Serena started to tremble as she realised that her deadly husband had outmanoeuvred her yet again.

'Oh, yes, that's right,' Nick said tightly. 'I got here first. Monique caught a cab and my chauffeur put his foot down. I've been in my bedroom since you first walked in.' He laughed under his breath, enjoying their appalled stares. 'Of course, one shouldn't eavesdrop. One so rarely hears anything good about oneself. But your conversation was so interesting that I simply couldn't bring myself to do the decent thing.'

Serena was immobile, staring at him as her breathing constricted, and her mind raced back over what she had said to Phil, wincing at every damning word.

'You listened...' Phil said in slow disbelief. 'To all of that...'

'Every last sentence,' Nick said through his teeth. 'I was interested to see how far you would go. Thought I'd give you plenty of rope, Greyson, and you really hanged yourself from the chandeliers didn't you?'

Phil was white, breathing thickly as he sprawled on his back at Nick's feet, half resting against the chair.

'I take it you have the perfect divorce lawyer,' Nick said in a frighteningly soft voice, 'just waiting to accept my wife's case?'

Phil's face ran with a tide of dark red colour and he flicked a quick guilty look at Serena, telling her in that moment that Nick was absolutely right, and she was appalled to realise that Phil had obviously had this in mind since he'd met her.

'While you prepare yourself, no doubt,' said Nick tightly, 'to play the role of supportive lover, holding her hand as she sobs into her handkerchief for the judge?'

Phil went scarlet, and Serena wanted to curl up and die. How could Phil be so underhand, so devious, so manipulative? She had thought he was her friend.

'All calculated, in fact,' Nick said bitingly, 'to destroy me. But I'm not going to let that happen, and do you know why?' Suddenly, his hands shot to Phil's lapels, lifting him to his feet, blue eyes blazing with rage. 'Because I'm going to destroy *you*!'

'No!' Phil stared, his face bleached white, cowering away from Nick.

'I can do it just by snapping my fingers, Greyson, and don't you forget it!' Nick snarled.

'Please!' Phil had his hands up in self-defence. 'It wasn't like that. I was trying to help Serena...I love her...I'm her friend...'

'Lady Serena to you!' Nick bit out. 'As for your claim to love her—look at her face. Do you really think she believes that pile of sentimental rubbish?'

Phil reddened, breathing hoarsely, glancing guiltily at Serena. 'All right...it's not true...I've been a fool, but for God's sake, Colterne—don't annihilate me for one stupid mistake.'

Nick studied him, his upper lip curled back in a sneer. 'What a guy! What a hero!'

'Please!' Phil's voice pleaded hoarsely.

There was a brief silence while Nick studied him with contempt. 'All right, Greyson—here's the deal,' he said through his teeth. 'You keep away from my wife, or I hack you up and turn you into pâté. Got that?'

'Yes.' Phil nodded. 'Is that all?'

'Almost,' Nick drawled menacingly, lifting his dark head, blue eyes deadly. 'You've learned a thing or two about my private life tonight...'

'It won't be repeated,' Phil said at once. 'I won't tell anyone anything. Nothing, Colterne. Not a damned thing.'

'I hope for your sake you don't,' Nick said tightly.

'I'd have to be mad to tell anyone in this town!' Phil said urgently. 'You must believe me! I really won't say a thing! Nothing at all...'

Nick studied him, his mouth hard, then he gave a cool nod. 'The door's over there. Use it.'

Phil swallowed, raked a hand through his blond hair and looked at Serena. There was a brief silence while they looked at each other, and she felt compassion for his humiliation at Nick's hands, but she also felt very angry at what he had tried to do.

He looked at her for a moment more, then turned and walked silently to the door. Nick watched him go, his face unreadable. The door closed behind him.

'Well,' Nick said tightly, swinging round on Serena. 'I think you've got a lot of explaining to do. Start now and make it good.'

Serena swallowed hard. 'You said you were going home with Monique. What did you expect me to do? Just come back here on my own?'

'Why not?' he asked flatly. 'You've done it a million times before. I've always had mistresses. What made tonight different for you?'

Anger flared in her eyes. 'It was too public! I felt humiliated. That's why you did it. It was deliberate. You wanted to get back at me for—'

'For going out with another man,' he bit out, leaning towards her, blue eyes blazing. 'And just why *did* you bring him back here with you, Serena? I'll tell you, shall I? You were playing tit-for-tat. You wanted to get back at me by sleeping with that bastard before—'

'That's not true!' She got to her feet, breathing hard. 'You must know it's not! You were listening in the bedroom. You must have heard everything I said, every word, every—'

'I'm not the CIA, Serena,' he cut in harshly. 'I

didn't bug the goddamned flat. I just listened at a door—I didn't hear everything.'

Her heart was beating very fast. 'You didn't hear everything?' Her voice seemed throaty, strangely weak. 'What exactly did you hear?'

His mouth tightened. 'Greyson's voice carries. Yours doesn't. I heard everything he said—nothing you said.' He looked her up and down, his blue eyes furious. 'You're going to have to fill me in on all those replies of yours, Serena, because I missed every last one of them, and I want to hear them. Right now.'

Relief swamped her, and she closed her eyes, breathing easier. He hadn't heard her say she wouldn't divorce him. He didn't know how deep her feelings went for him. Neither did she. She didn't understand why she felt such a powerful loyalty towards him, but at least she was spared the humiliation of his knowing.

'Answer me.' His hand caught her chin, forcing her to face him, his eyes brutal. 'What did my loving wife say when asked to take me to the cleaners and sue me to the hilt?'

Serena gave a hoarse, ironic laugh.

'Don't you laugh at me, you little bitch!' he said through his teeth, fingers tightening like a vice on her chin. 'I can assure you I wouldn't go meekly to the slaughter. You'd have to put a gun to my head to get me to the divorce courts, let alone the cleaners. I'd take you to hell and back before I let you do that to me.'

'Would you, Nick?' she whispered. 'I thought we were already there?'

'Not just yet, baby!' His mouth shook. 'You haven't

burnt in hell-fire until you've fought me face to face. Don't even think about divorce. I'd kill you...I'd really take the gloves off with you, Serena,' he said thickly. 'You'd be punch-drunk before you even got to the lawyer's office.'

She shivered, then said shakily, 'I believe you, Nick. But that doesn't mean I can't consider my options. Divorce was inevitably going to rear its ugly head between us.'

'And I'll cut it off,' he said, biting out the words. 'I protect what's mine, Serena. Regardless of how or why—you're one of my possessions and I intend to keep you. If that means I have to punch every man who comes near you then I'll do it.'

Bitterly, she said, 'My knight in shining armour!'

'Just think of me as the Black Prince,' he drawled maliciously.

'I'm trapped, then?' she whispered, hating him. 'Divorce isn't even an option for me?'

'Not while there's life left in my body,' he said thickly. 'I'll never let you go.'

'You couldn't stop me.' Tears stung her eyes. 'Not if I were determined.'

The blue eyes narrowed. 'Are you determined, Serena?'

She lowered her gaze from him, her lashes sweeping the vulnerable curve of her cheek, and did not reply. She wouldn't lie to him. But she certainly wouldn't tell him the truth.

Bitterly, she smiled and said, 'I'd have to be mad to try and fight you. All I can do now is live with a man I hate, and who hates me. Is that the kind of marriage you want?'

He gave a hard smile. 'It seems to be the kind of marriage I've got.'

'Doesn't that bother you?' she whispered.

'Not if I get an heir from you,' he drawled softly.

Serena shivered, staring at his deadly face, and her voice said shakily, 'My father's accountant described you as a ruthless shark the day he first mentioned your name. He was right, wasn't he? I didn't realise it fully until now.' Her eyes traced his hard face. 'But that's what you are, isn't it? You really don't give a damn what you destroy or who you hurt or how many people you trample on. So long as you get what you want in the end—you're satisfied.'

A hard smile touched his mouth. 'But I haven't got what I want yet, have I? And until I do the lessons you're learning will just get tougher and tougher, Serena, until one day…you just submit.'

'Submission…' she said hoarsely. 'That's the key, is it? You want to totally possess me, crush my spirit, make me surrender completely.'

'That's generally what happens at the end of a war,' he said.

He released her suddenly, striding arrogantly to the drinks cabinet. Serena watched him through her lashes, bitterly aware that their marriage was now nailed out in grim reality for them both to see. A war…a lesson in submission…how she hated him.

Why did I refuse to divorce him? she thought bitterly. I must have been mad. If I had any sense I'd walk out now and start to fight him, sue him to the hilt, drag him through the mud, besmirch his reputation in Boston and the rest of the world...

A painful sigh wrenched her as she realised she couldn't do it. Just couldn't contemplate it. The loyalty she felt towards him was stronger, if anything, than it had been when Phil first asked her to divorce.

Why did she feel this deep loyalty to Nick? Why...? It just didn't make sense.

Nick turned, whisky glass in hand. The blue eyes ran coolly over her. 'So,' he drawled, 'I think we're beginning to understand one another.'

'As well as we ever can,' she said thickly. 'I ought to thank you for opening my eyes to your true nature. I always knew you were a ruthless bastard—I just hadn't guessed at the appalling extent of it.'

Nick watched her with cynical mockery. 'My innocent little wife. You'd better stay that way, or I'll have your head on a plate.' His voice hardened suddenly. 'If I ever catch Greyson or others like him anywhere near you, Serena, I'll turn very nasty indeed. Do I make myself clear?'

'As crystal,' she said thickly, looking up. 'And what of your mistresses? Does the situation continue as it always has? Or are you going to make my life unbearable by flaunting them in front of me?'

He walked coolly to her, smiling mockingly down at her. His hand slid to her naked throat. 'Jealous, Serena?'

Angrily, she dashed his hand away. 'I can't stand the sight of you! Why should I be jealous?'

'You can't stand the sight of me,' he repeated under

his breath, blue eyes narrowing. He looked her up and down, then said tightly, 'Get on the couch.'

She caught her breath, heart missing a beat. 'No...'

He smiled tightly and then took her wrist in a hard grip, pulling her over to the couch while she struggled, heart banging in her breast, whispering humiliating pleas for him to stop.

'Don't...don't...!' She stumbled as he reached the couch, and flung her down on it on her back. Winded, she struggled to sit up, but he was already slamming his whisky glass down on the side-table and sliding on top of her. 'Nick, please...'

'You little bitch!' he said hoarsely, hands pinning her to the couch. 'You let him kiss you, touch you...you let him stand there and talk about destroying me—and then you tell me to my face that you can't stand the sight of me!' His hard body crushed hers, his ruthless mouth inches from hers. 'Do you really expect me to be nice to you after that?'

'You've never been nice to me,' she whispered, heart slamming as she felt those hard thighs trapping hers beneath him. 'I sometimes wonder if you married me in order to punish me.'

'I didn't,' he said thickly. 'But I sure as hell intend to now!' His mouth touched hers angrily, pushing her lips apart as she struggled, making him angrier until his mouth became brutal, bruising her soft lips and making her give cries of hurt and anger.

He was deliberately punishing with his kiss, inflicting pain, his fingers hard around her wrists as he pinned her beneath him. Serena struggled violently, trying to slap him, scratch at him, but he was too strong for her, she couldn't even lift her hands from the couch, and her kicking legs were completely restricted by his.

He laughed at her, blue eyes blazing as his mouth grew more demanding, more punishing.

'You're hurting me!' she moaned hoarsely through bruised lips.

'I want to hurt you,' he said thickly. 'Sometimes I'd like to kill you, Serena.' He stared down at her, his heart thudding loudly, and whispered, 'Sometimes I'd like to kill you!'

They stared at each other for a long moment, and there was blood on her lips, but her heart was pounding very fast and heated excitement was pumping through her body.

'I'd like to kill you, too, Nick!' she whispered passionately, green eyes blazing. 'I've never hated anyone as much as I hate you and I can't stand it any longer...I can't stand it!'

Nick gave a sudden rough sound of excitement, and then he was kissing her until her head span, his mouth hot and searingly exciting, sending waves of sensual pleasure through Serena as he released her wrists, his hands sliding to her body, and she needed to express her violent feelings so much that she found her hands moving to his strong neck, her fingers shaking as they thrust into his black hair, her mouth parting passionately beneath his, kissing him back with fierce emotion all blending into one dazzling explosion of desire made from anger, hatred, long-buried need...

His hands were moving over her, sliding up to close

over her full breasts, and she arched against him with a hoarse cry, her nipples already fiercely erect.

Dizzy, drowning in the grip of primitive excitement, she offered her neck to him, whispering angry words of hatred as he kissed her throat where the pulse beat so hotly, clutching his dark head to her, moaning out loud as she felt him part her thighs with one hard leg and slide his strong hands down to cup her rear.

'I hate you!' she whispered, running her hands over his broad shoulders. 'Kiss me...'

His mouth came back to hers, demanding and hungry, and her body was arching against him as that heartbeat deafened her, slamming violently above her; she realised suddenly that it was Nick's heart, so she slid her shaking hands to his hard-muscled chest and felt the heavy thudding against her fingers as she clung to his ruthless mouth, kissing him blindly, her eyes closed and her body like liquid fire in his arms.

Nick raised his head, darkly flushed and breathing harshly. 'Come to bed...'

It was like a slap in the face. She froze, rigid suddenly beneath him, all the passion draining from her as the colour left her face and she realised what she had done.

'No,' she said in a small, hoarse voice. 'Let me go...I shouldn't have done that...I didn't know what I was doing...I—'

He held her down as she tried to get away. 'You knew what you were doing,' he said under his breath. 'You've spent three years married to a man you want without ever letting him make love to you. My God, how much more frustration can you take, Serena? No

wonder you blew a fuse just now. Don't try to deny
it, or run from it. Come to bed with me now and let's
end this war once and for all.'

'Go to hell!' Serena shook as she stared at him.

'You want me,' he said raggedly, his hand moving
over her aching breast. 'Tell me…say it…'

Hot colour burnt her face and she said in angry denial, 'I don't want you, Nick. I only kissed you back
because I'd been driven half crazy with rage and I
wanted to show it to you…take it out on you…'

'That's exactly what I want you to do,' he said under his breath. 'In bed. I want you to take it out on
me…all of it, Serena…'

'Well, I won't!' she said fiercely, tears stinging her
eyes. 'Not willingly, Nick! The situation hasn't
changed—can't you understand that? It doesn't make
any difference how long you've stayed away. It could
be three years or thirty-three! I still wouldn't let you
make love to me under these circumstances. Not ever.'
Her eyes blazed. 'You can force me to give you an
heir if you really want to, but I'll make it as difficult
as possible for you. I'll fight you, Nick, just as I did
on our wedding night. And if you take me I'll scratch
your face to ribbons.'

He studied her for a second in tense silence. Menace
glittered in his eyes. 'I see,' he drawled with a dangerous smile. 'It's going to be a long and bitter war,
then, before your ultimate surrender?'

'There won't be a surrender,' she said fiercely. 'Not
ever, Nick.'

'Don't kid yourself, Serena,' he mocked softly. 'I
almost had you just now. If I'd been prepared to take

you here on the couch you would have been mine before you started to fight.'

Her face flamed. 'Now who's kidding who? No man has ever seen me naked, Nick Colterne. I'd certainly notice if you were the first!'

He laughed under his breath. 'You have a point. An idiotic one, but a point.' The blue eyes narrowed on her flushed face. 'Which leaves me looking for a new strategy. I'm not making love to you until you admit you want me.'

'Why should you care if I want you or not?' she asked bitterly.

'Because I find victory exciting,' he drawled softly. 'And you've been fighting me for three years. I shall relish your absolute defeat.'

Serena winced, her face white.

He smiled at her appalled expression. 'But I think I'll enjoy it even more if I conquer you on your own home territory.' He laughed softly. 'My defeated little aristocrat, surrendering where it all began three years ago.' He lifted his dark ruthless head. 'In Flaxton Manor. We leave tomorrow.'

CHAPTER SIX

NICK'S private jet flew them to London the following afternoon. Serena sat beside him, her slender body expensively dressed in pale cream silk, intensely feminine, her long red-gold hair a silk cluster of waves falling to her waist.

Through her seductive hairstyle, her slanting green eyes watched Nick's hard face as he sat beside her, every inch the ruthless tycoon, the cynical line of his mouth devastatingly attractive to her. The thought of his ultimate conquest of her was beginning to take root in her, exciting her against her will, making her hate him even more than she had done for three years. How could a man like this make her want him, even when he was deliberately cruel to her? What made the situation even more unbearable was knowing that she would never, could never let him make love to her without love...

'We'll stay overnight at the London house,' Nick told her coolly as they flew across the glittering azure Atlantic. 'I've arranged an appointment with Sir Charles Warwick.'

'But he's the most respected art dealer in England!' she said with a sharp frown. 'You're going to a lot of trouble...'

'You're one of my assets, Serena,' he said flatly. 'I shall enjoy having an aristocratic English wife who is also a talented and respected artist. Sir Charles will be calling at the house at six tonight for drinks and dinner.'

'You certainly aren't wasting any time,' she said bitterly.

'I always move quickly,' he said, arching black brows. 'As you'll find out at Flaxton Manor.'

Excitement pulsed treacherously in her veins, but she fought it. 'You mean you're planning to take me to bed the first night we get there? How very exciting for me! I simply can't wait!' Sarcasm blazed in her eyes. 'What will you do when I start to fight? Tie me to the bed?'

'What an interesting idea,' he drawled sardonically.

'You obviously don't realise I'm serious,' she said tightly.

Nick gave her a cool smile. 'Neither do you believe it of me. But I don't talk idly of surrender and conquest, Serena. By the time we leave Flaxton Manor, I can assure you, you will almost certainly be not only my lover, but also—with any luck—pregnant.'

Serena jerked her face from him, staring unseeingly at the dove-grey walls of the private jet. How she hated him. Hated her own fierce response to him. The thought of arriving at Flaxton Manor suddenly filled her with dread. If he carried out his threat, she would have to fight. What other option did she have? She couldn't possibly let him make love to her. Not knowing he was only using her, using her body for sexual pleasure and for getting an heir. It didn't bear thinking about...

Her hand shook as she lifted her drink to her lips. It would be a bitter struggle between them, but she was determined. Nick Colterne would never find her a willing lover. Never.

They touched down at Heathrow. Whisked through Customs and passport control, they were met by a chauffeur and Rolls-Royce limousine, which sped through the elegant streets of Knightsbridge towards their house in Bellamy Square, Mayfair.

'Welcome home, sir, my lady!' Chivers, the butler, opened the elegant white door with a bright smile. 'Oh, how lovely to have you back with us!'

'Hello, Chivers!' Serena gave him a warm look through her lashes. 'Did Mrs Chivers find the cat in the end?'

'Yes, my lady.' Chivers closed the door and picked up their suitcases, his eyes filled with laughter. 'Trapped in the spare bedroom, clawing at the door and kicking up a terrible fuss!'

Serena smiled. 'It's good to be back...'

Nick looked at his watch, white cuffs shooting back with the movement to show the Rolex on his hard, hair-roughened wrist. 'It's almost four. You'd better take a bath and get ready to impress Sir Charles.'

Serena nodded, and went upstairs to her bedroom. It was as elegant and beautiful as all her other bedrooms all over the world. Nick had chosen the décor, of course, and the intense femininity of the cream walls, cream and gold antique furniture and deep-pile beige carpet were echoed by the ravishing four-poster bed with its thick velvet curtains in rich cream.

In the warm, flowered bathroom, Serena relaxed in the scented steam. It was the first time for months that they had both been in the house together. A prickle of deep awareness ran over her naked body. She closed her eyes, wondering what would happen, how she would cope, when he decided it was time to take her to bed...

The thought of it made her tremble, her skin flushing delicate pink. Getting out of the bath, she wrapped herself in a fluffy green bathrobe and padded barefoot and wet-haired into the bedroom.

Nick was lounging indolently on the bed.

Her heart stopped and she halted, staring at him, feeling his blue eyes move with stark sexual appraisal over her as her heart began to pound a fierce rhythm and the flood of hot colour surged into her face.

'What are you doing here...?' she whispered thickly, although she knew, and felt defenceless, deeply aware of her nudity beneath the bathrobe.

Nick got to his feet. 'I came to see you.'

She backed, suddenly feeling very vulnerable indeed.

'You said you'd wait...not until Flaxton Manor, you said...'

He walked towards her, his eyes dark with intent, and she started to shake, unable to move away from him, her green eyes enormous whirlpools of hunger in her flushed face.

'I want to see you,' he said under his breath, and his hands slowly loosened the belt of her robe.

'No!' she protested, stopping his hand.

He tugged on the belt and the robe fell open. Serena struggled bitterly, but he was implacable, his mouth a tough line.

'Stand still, Serena,' he commanded, and pulled the robe open to expose her.

'Oh, God…!' she whispered, closing her eyes, helpless, dazed, her heart thumping violently, appalled at her vulnerability as she felt his blue eyes burning over her naked body.

'You're beautiful,' his voice said thickly, and when his strong hands slid to her naked waist she opened her eyes and stared at him with violent hunger. Slowly, he lowered his dark head to kiss her shaking mouth and the passion swept them together immediately. Her hands clung to his shoulders, her mouth opening beneath the hot onslaught of his kiss, and when he ran his hands over her naked body she moaned, shivering with desire, squirming away from him, angrily aware that she loved the feel of his hands on her.

'I'm no match for you like this,' she moaned against his mouth. 'But I'll still fight if you try to take me.'

'Why?' he asked thickly, raising his flushed face an inch from hers, his mouth almost touching hers. 'You want me, Serena, and your desire gets stronger every time I kiss you.'

'Desire?' she whispered through love-bruised lips. 'What's desire when it's fuelled by hatred instead of love?'

'Infinitely more exciting,' he said softly, kissing her.

'No.' She ran her hands over his hateful, strong neck. 'It's not lovemaking at all, Nick. That's why the phrase was coined, isn't it? To make love is to be in love, and we hardly qualify.'

'Is that what you think? That you can't make love without being in love? I must teach you how exciting lovemaking can be when you just let go of childish illusions and satisfy adult demands…'

His hard mouth closed over hers, making her moan in heated response, hating him, her hands pushing at his broad shoulders, but her naked body was trembling, flushed with hot colour as he pressed her against his hard male body, and the desire was suddenly flooding her veins like fire.

The strong hands moved expertly over her, wringing tortuous pleasure where they touched, caressing her bare breasts, sliding down to cup her rear, pressing her sensually against his hardness.

'I want you like hell!' he bit out thickly, hands shaking on her slender naked thighs. 'Come to bed…submit…'

'No…' she whispered thickly, her hands in his dark hair as her mouth moved passionately against his and her body was like pale fire against his masculine body. 'Never…'

His hands were parting her thighs, her gasps turning to hoarse cries, and as she heard the rough gasp of excitement from the back of his throat she felt the increased pressure on her mouth, felt those hands move higher, sending the sweet rush of excitement through her.

'No!' she said with sudden, violent determination, and dragged herself from him. 'I won't let you do it, you bastard! You think you can coax me into it because my body is weak, but my mind is stronger, Nick!' Her eyes blazed. 'I'll fight you to the end!'

He looked at her, mocking triumph in his eyes. 'But each time I touch you, we go just a little bit further. Once it was just a kiss. Then a touch. Now I have you naked. What do you think will be next?' He smiled at her shocked expression, then released her, running a hand through his dark hair as he strode coolly to the door. 'I can stand the pressure,' he said softly. 'Can you?' With a cynical smile he left, the door closing quietly behind him.

Serena was shaking so hard that she could barely stand up. Stunned, dazed, she groped her way to the bed and sank on to it, her heart thundering through her body, blood pulsing in her veins like wildfire.

He was right. Her own desire for him was becoming too strong. Just being with him twenty-four hours a day, with his incessant battering at her resistance, would eventually obliterate her defences…and then he would take her. Only then…when her desire had become intolerable. When it had gone beyond red-hot and was burning white.

How could she continue to fight him? Hot tears stung her eyes. She dashed them away angrily. I'll have to be strong, she told herself. I mustn't let him take me without a fight…

Later, she dressed in a pale powder-blue silk shift dress, its contours skimming her slender curves with exquisite elegance, her long red-gold hair blow-dried in her usual style, and her green slanting eyes emphasised with a hint of liner.

Going downstairs just before six, she walked into

the study and found Nick already there, arranging her paintings carefully, the packing cases almost empty and standing in the corner.

'Oh…!' Serena hesitated in the doorway, her eyes racing over his powerful frame, devastatingly sexy in the impeccable grey Savile Row suit he wore. 'My paintings…'

'Time was cutting close,' he drawled, straightening. 'I thought I'd better get them set out in case he arrived early.'

'How very efficient of you,' she said, lifting red-gold brows.

He gave a lazy, cynical smile. 'Glad you're thrilled.'

The doorbell rang.

'That'll be him,' Nick said coolly, putting the painting down as the centre-piece on the long mahogany table. 'Come on. Let's get this show on the road.'

He strode ahead of her into the drawing-room. He dominated the elegant room, as he dominated every room, and Serena followed him in, her eyes wary, running over his powerful body, intensely aware of him, of his wicked mind, his ruthless mouth and his irresistible sex appeal.

Did she even stand a chance against him? She already half wanted to surrender…she closed her eyes, turning from him, sinking into an armchair, willing herself to be strong.

'Sir Charles Warwick,' Chivers announced a moment later.

'Charles!' Nick swung from the cool Adam fireplace, strode to Sir Charles, extending a hand. 'Good to see you! Come in…'

'My dear chap.' Sir Charles was an elegant, charming and very dignified man with silver hair and intelligent grey eyes. 'The pleasure is all mine!'

The two men shook hands with firm grips, respect in each other's smiles as they faced each other.

'And you have your lovely wife at your side!' Sir Charles turned to Serena, smiling. 'Marvellous to see you again, my dear.'

'Hello, Sir Charles.' Serena kissed his austere cheek. 'How's Lady Warwick?'

'Plotting to spring another garden party on me!' he groaned. 'How I hate all the work that leads up to them! Women everywhere, arranging flowers and baking cakes…!'

Serena laughed. 'Hide in your study until the guests arrive! That's what my father always does!'

'A drink, Charles?' Nick drawled from the cabinet. 'Whisky?'

'On ice.' Sir Charles laughed, thrusting his hands in the pockets of his light grey suit. 'I do love Americanisms. They're so modern, and my children frequently accuse me of being what they call a ''branflake-eater''. Apparently, this is the ultimate in old age.'

Nick handed him his whisky, his body movements as quick and mercurial as always. 'I shan't sympathise, Charles. Personally, I'm looking forward to being a father.'

Serena stared at him through her lashes as the words slid into her heart. Children…it was becoming a greater reality than ever. She was helpless to prevent what was going to happen.

'Oh?' Sir Charles's silver brows rose as he glanced at Serena.

A smile touched Nick's hard mouth. 'Come and see my wife's paintings, Charles,' he drawled coolly, striding towards the door. 'They really are quite exceptionally good.'

Sir Charles let his gaze linger on Serena for a few seconds, then turned and followed Nick.

In the study, Sir Charles inspected the paintings with a cool, professional eye. He was silent, moving along the mahogany table, his austere face stern.

Serena could hardly bear to wait for his judgement. Tense, she braced herself for a possible rejection. Sir Charles wouldn't lie to her. Not only that, but he wouldn't be interested in her name and background as selling points. All he was interested in was artistic merit.

Nick was standing beside her, his face hard, hands thrust in grey trouser-pockets, authority in every line of his body. Suddenly she knew he was tense, too.

Sir Charles turned at last, his face cool.

'Well?' Nick asked tersely.

Sir Charles arched silver brows. 'Well, I must admit I'm surprised at the style. A cross between primitive and Impressionist, with a touch of Van Gogh in the skies.'

'And?' Nick arched black brows.

'And I think an exhibition should be arranged at once.' Sir Charles flicked his grey gaze to Serena's face, and he was thoughtful, studying her with new eyes. 'Well done, my dear. I think you have a very promising future.'

Serena couldn't speak for a second, then managed to choke out a husky, 'Thank you...!'

'You'll have to keep it up, though,' Sir Charles warned sternly. 'One exhibition won't be enough. The art world isn't interested in people who make a big splash, a lot of money, and then disappear. Either you continue to paint, grow and develop—or forget it.'

Serena felt a little daunted by that, suddenly realising the commitment she would have to make, but at the same time she could not bring herself to let go of that intense, obsessive little world she had carved for herself.

Nick would still be away frequently on business, even if she did find herself pregnant at some time in the future. She knew she would rely heavily on her easel and paints in his absence. What else would she have in her life? she thought bitterly. Nick was clearly determined to isolate her again.

Dinner was a fascinating affair. They talked about art, finance, London, high society and children. Serena noticed Nick watching her with a cool smile, a gleam in his blue eyes as he listened to her talk so articulately, gesturing with slim hands, her face mercurial, her mind quicksilver as Sir Charles listened intently and joined in.

'Wonderful evening!' Sir Charles said as he left, shaking hands firmly with Nick at the door. 'You must come to my wife's garden party and rescue me from raffle tickets! How long are you in England for?'

'I'm not sure yet,' Nick said coolly, shrugging broad shoulders. 'But I'll let you know.'

Sir Charles nodded and kissed Serena. 'Give my regards to your parents, my dear. Tell them their invitations to the garden party are in the post.'

When he had gone Nick looked down at Serena with a cool smile. Her heart skipped several beats at the look in his eyes, especially when they slid to her full mouth.

'You're a success,' he drawled, a sardonic smile on his mouth. 'How does it feel?'

'It feels good. But it would feel much better if I had secured it for myself.'

His smile grew cynical. 'You had your chance and you blew it.'

'You mean you blew it for me,' she returned, arching red-gold brows. 'You blew it sky-high!'

He laughed softly, blue eyes moving over her. 'I'm an explosive kind of guy.' His strong hand moved to her throat. 'That's why you can't resist me when I put the pressure on.'

'Your conceit is even greater than your arrogance.'

'Justified arrogance,' he said softly, 'can be intolerably exciting. Don't you think?' His dark head bent, and as his mouth met hers she gave a moan of pleasure, her lips parting swiftly beneath his. He was pulling her into his arms, and she went willingly, her hands clasping his strong throat as the kiss deepened. She could pull away...when she wanted to...but for now she wanted his mouth on hers...

Her eyes closed in helpless response, expecting to feel his hands on her body, longing for that wicked seduction to begin, her heart thumping violently as she twined against him, hating him, wanting him...

Suddenly, she was released.

Swaying, she stared hotly through her lashes, her mouth still moist and receptive, not understanding why he had ended the kiss.

'Goodnight, Serena!' Nick drawled in soft mockery, and turned on his heel, striding towards the stairs.

Hot colour flooded her face. Humiliated, bitterly angry, she could only catch her breath and choke back her fury as she stared after him and his cool, arrogant stride. Only when he had disappeared from sight did she put her hands to her hot face and close her eyes, wincing at the depths of her humiliation.

He knew now...he knew...oh, she felt such a fool. How could he have done that to her? How? Rage shot through her. Well, it wouldn't get him anywhere, she vowed furiously. She might have wanted that kiss to go on, but she certainly wouldn't have allowed it to lead to lovemaking. Nor would she allow any kisses in the future to lead to that. If he thought he could drive her into bed with taunting, mockery and frustration, he could think again!

Next morning they drove to Flaxton.

The manor gates rose in front of them, clean white stone with the Flaxton crest in shining red and gold, the Boleyn crest on the opposite pillar, and twin stone unicorns rising up holding those shields.

The sign beside the gate listed the hours of public opening, and the guard stepped out of his little blue hut to bend to the window. His eyes widened in surprise when he peered into the rear window of the limousine. 'Oh, I'm sorry, my lady!' he said, smiling at Serena. 'Didn't recognise the car for a minute. Go right through; they're expecting you.'

The limousine slid through the extensive parkland, and Serena studied it with pride as she always did, delighted with the changes in the estate since Nick took it over. The land had once been wild and unruly; now it was landscaped, mown to perfection with deer grazing on it, the lake a lovely wild vision on the horizon.

Tourists were milling about in front of the manor. Its Tudor chimneys rose like barley sugar, the turrets of each wing resembling the Tower of London, and the red brick walls kept clean and shining as new.

The car park was packed with cars, the café was doing a roaring trade behind the stables, and the gift shop seemed to have mushroomed to three times its original size.

'Your father's garden centre was a good idea,' Nick observed as they drove past the public apartments. 'Look at all those cars in front of it. I hear he's even started importing stone garden statues from China…'

'Yes, he mentioned that at Christmas,' Serena said, studying the long glass house on the far side of the manor. 'But he's got a way with gardens, plants, landscaping.'

'We'll have to call him Capability Flaxton,' Nick drawled, shooting her a glance.

'He'd be thrilled if you did!' she said, thinking of her father's long admiration for Capability Brown, the greatest British landscape gardener of all time.

The limousine drove around the curving drive to the private gates of her parents' private wing. The guard waved them through, and they slid up with a crunch of gravel to the West Wing.

Mottram answered the door. 'Hello, my lady,' she said with a slight bob, her black and white maid's uniform starched to within an inch of its life. 'Mr Colterne, sir. Lovely to have you back. Your apartments are ready, and the Countess is serving tea in the drawing-room in ten minutes.'

Nick and Serena had a brief chat with Mottram about life at Flaxton Manor since Christmas, and heard all about the latest scandal ricocheting around the staff.

'She got pregnant and eloped to Australia with him.' Mottram was aflush with excitement, leading Nick and Serena up the carved wooden stairs to their apartments. 'We got a postcard from her this morning...'

'Has she had the baby yet?' Serena asked, agog.

'Oh, no, she was only three months gone when they went!'

As they entered their apartments Serena gave a sigh and kicked off her high heels. 'I'm exhausted!'

Nick thanked the chauffeur for bringing their cases, and gave him the rest of the day off, aware that he had taken a fancy to Mottram and would go off in hot pursuit.

'Home at last!' Nick stretched, flexing those powerful shoulder muscles, and Serena studied him through her lashes, her mouth dry. He straightened, caught her secretly admiring gaze, and a sardonic smile touched his hard mouth as he turned, drawling, 'Shall we unpack? Or do you want to go straight to bed?'

She flushed, aware that he had seen the desire in her eyes in that unguarded moment, and hating him for his quick, clever mind. 'I'll unpack!' she said flatly, and went into her bedroom.

Nick followed her lazily in, put her suitcase on the floor.

Serena turned, deeply aware of him, and her heart started to beat with abrupt violence at the look in his eyes.

'Do you still have that dress?' he asked softly.

'What dress?'

'You know which dress I mean,' he said, his eyes mocking. 'See if you can find it. I might want to make love to you tonight, and I'd like you to be wearing it when I do.'

He turned, leaving the room, the door closing behind him with a cool click, leaving Serena angrily breathless, her pulses racing, her body shaking with a desire that went so deep that she could barely stand to live with it unsated any more.

Dry-mouthed, she sank on to the bed. Did he mean it? He might make love to her tonight? Oh, God...her body was throbbing with a need she hated herself for feeling.

Struggling to come to terms with the dynamic shift in their relationship, Serena drew a long unsteady breath, telling herself this was all just nonsense, she didn't want him to make love to her, he was a ruthless bastard and she hated him...

Getting to her feet, she unpacked, ignoring the tremor in her hands as she hung her expensive dresses in the wardrobe. The bedroom was as familiar to her now as her old room in the Queen's apartments had been when she first met Nick. Of course, the Queen's

apartments were now on show to the public. Anne
Boleyn's frequent visits to Flaxton Manor were one
of the most famous aspects of the house, and a
big draw for the public, particularly combined with
Henry VIII's apartments.

The sun glinted through the lattice windows, casting
diamond light on the old four-poster bed with its bright
new red velvet curtains and handmade patchwork
quilt.

Suddenly, she remembered the wooden drawers below that bed, and went to them, thinking, I wonder...

Kneeling, she pulled out a rickety drawer, rifled
through the memorabilia from her teens, and there was
the dress, at the bottom of the drawer, the demure lace
dress she had first worn when she met Nick Colterne
three years ago...

The knock at the door made her jump, turning.

Nick opened the door slowly, and saw her kneeling
on the floor, the dress in her hands and a fierce hot
rush of colour rising to her cheeks as she looked up
guiltily.

He stared at her in tense silence. Then he crossed
the room to her in three strides, taking her shoulders
in hard hands and lifting her. 'Put it on for me!' he
said thickly, hands sliding to her waist, pulling her
hard against him. 'Put it on and let me take it off.'

'No!' she said fiercely, aware that she desperately
wanted to do as he commanded, and also aware that
the war was no longer just between her and Nick: it
was now breaking out inside her as she fought her own
desire. 'I don't want to put it on for you, and I cer-

tainly wouldn't let you take it off! Besides—my mother's waiting and I—'

'So am I,' he bit out thickly. 'I've been waiting for three damned years! Let me see you in it...'

'My mother is waiting downstairs for us,' she said again. 'Do you really want to start this now? I'll fight you, Nick. Do you want to go downstairs in an hour with another scratch on your face?'

'I wouldn't mind going down with a few scratches on my back,' he drawled sardonically, then drew a harsh breath, releasing her. 'Very well. But put the damned dress down and come out of the bedroom immediately, or I won't be answerable for the consequences.'

Silent, ashen, she pushed the dress on to the bed and walked out of the bedroom. He watched her pass with brooding eyes. She felt his intent gaze on her body and quivered inwardly, her heart pounding.

'Before we go down to your mother, though,' Nick said coolly, following her into the drawing-room, 'I think we should discuss the finer points of your new life in respect to them.'

Serena turned, green eyes wary. 'What do you mean?'

'Your art,' he said sardonically, and thrust his hands into his trouser-pockets, the stance of masculine authority deeply exciting to her. 'This is the time to tell them, Serena. Now or never. You've just been accepted for a major exhibition at one of the top galleries in London. If you don't tell both your parents about it now, they'll find out themselves, and then your opportunity will be lost.'

She frowned, folded her arms, green eyes even more wary. 'I don't see that they have to know at all.'

He laughed. 'Come off it. And quit being so secretive. It's time you grew out of it.'

'I'm not secretive,' she denied angrily, stiffening.

'Oh, yes, you are,' he said coolly, arching black brows. 'And it's got to stop. Particularly with me. But the first step is with your parents. They made you secretive, not me—and that's where you've got to break the pattern. By telling them point-blank what you're really doing with your life.'

'Well, I...' She broke off, staring at him, as his words struck home. It was true. She had always been secretive with her parents, because she had always known they wouldn't understand anything she wanted to do. More than that—they weren't really interested. After the first few rebuffs, she had simply shut off from them, guarding everything she did.

'They never understood you, did they?' Nick said softly, watching her. 'You were like some exotic bird of paradise living in their calm, quiet country world. You didn't even look like them, let alone think like them.'

Serena stared at him, her eyes pained. 'How did you know?' she asked huskily, then, 'I mean—how did you guess?'

'I always knew. It was just a question of letting you find out on your own.' He opened the door. 'Now come on. Time to break the spell and face the music.'

Serena walked to the door, prickling with awareness as she passed him.

'By the way,' Nick asked as they went downstairs,

'where did you actually paint? It couldn't have been at any of our homes, or I would have heard about it.'

'I hired a studio,' she confessed. 'One in London, one in New York.'

'And paid cash so I wouldn't find out,' he drawled sardonically. 'You devious little minx! I shall have to teach you interesting lessons in bed about what happens when my wife tries to deceive me.'

Breathless, she looked away. 'Is that all you think about?'

'It is since you found that demure little dress...' he mocked.

A second later they were downstairs, and Nick was opening the door and leading her in to find her mother sitting in an old armchair, the sun on her pale, powdery face, her ash-blonde hair pulled back in an untidy bun as she embroidered a cushion.

'Hello, darling!' Elizabeth, Countess Archallagen, rose in her slippered feet, looking just like a rambling old painting in her tweed skirt and cream twin set. 'Lovely to see you again. Must say, didn't expect a visit, but you young people live such extraordinary lives.'

The dogs lolloped over towards Serena and Nick. There were dog hairs everywhere, covering every piece of furniture, and piles of old piano music slithering off the even older piano.

'Oh, get down, you bad boys!' The Countess swiped the muzzle of a fat retriever. 'You'll spoil Serena's dress!' She pushed a stray hair back into her untidy bun. 'Where's the tea?' She walked to the door and

opened it. 'Mottram!' she bellowed as though at a
hunt. 'Bring the damned tea!'

Nick strolled with cool arrogance across the room,
leant against the fireplace, a thoughtful expression on
his face. He looked as out of place as Serena felt,
especially in that impeccable black suit, his air of sophistication and power so striking, every inch the ruthless tycoon with lethal sex appeal.

The Countess looked at him as though he were from
Mars. 'Don't loom, Nick, please! You make me feel
uncomfortable. Sit down—just push a dog off a chair
and relax.'

'Where's Papa?' Serena asked, studying her mother.

'Pottering about somewhere.' The Countess waved
a hand and sank back into her armchair. 'In the garden
centre, I shouldn't wonder. Well—to what do we owe
this privilege, my dear?'

Serena looked at Nick. He arched black brows at
her. She swallowed, turned to her mother. 'Well, we
came to England because I've sort of started a career,
I suppose…'

'A career?' Her mother picked up her embroidery.
'Oh, that's nice, dear.'

Serena grew more confident. 'I've been painting.
I'm an artist now. Well, sort of…' She told her mother
briefly about the meeting with Sir Charles.

'A garden party?' the Countess said with a smile.
'Oh, I must take one of my cheesecakes. Lady
Warwick will like that.'

The door opened and Mottram came in with a bob
and a tea-tray.

'So you're an artist now, are you dear?' The

Countess poured the tea a moment later, a smile on her powdery face. 'Well, you don't surprise me. Nothing surprises me about you any more.' She laughed. 'In fact, you've been a surprise from start to finish really, haven't you? We called you Serena because we thought you might bring some serenity into our middle and old age, but of course you didn't.' She sighed, her eyes affectionate as they flicked over her daughter's vivid red hair, slanting green eyes and sophisticated, sensual body, her sex appeal blazing out as it always did, almost oozing through the pores of her skin. 'You were always too powerful a personality to bring anyone serenity!'

CHAPTER SEVEN

LATER, the Earl came into the drawing-room, dressed in tweeds, pulling gardening gloves off his gnarled old hands, exclaiming heartily as he shook hands with Nick and kissed Serena with discomfort, staring at her pale cream silk shift dress in baffled admiration.

'Absolutely first class to see you!' he kept saying, standing by the fireplace, his moustache now quite white with age. 'Absolutely first class!'

'I see the garden centre's doing a roaring trade,' Nick drawled, his powerful presence the most dominant force in the room as he lounged coolly in the armchair next to Serena, his body like a jungle cat's.

'Yes, it is!' the Earl agreed. 'And the manor's in an uproar over this latest charity bash!'

'Charity bash?' Nick frowned.

'Didn't we tell you?' The Earl arched bushy silver brows. 'Yes, the RSPCA are holding a vast banquet there tonight. Celebrities and other odd types, all flying in to attend and write out cheques while under the influence.' He laughed gruffly, grey eyes alight. 'Best if you attend, too, of course, but not necessary if you can't face it.'

'I wish you'd told me.' Serena made a face. 'I don't think I packed anything suitable.'

'I think you packed that green evening dress, darling,' Nick said coolly beside her. 'I remember seeing it on the bed this morning.'

Her gaze shot to his face. 'Oh, yes!' She had had no idea he watched her so closely, observed her movements, noted down even the clothes she packed.

After tea, Serena and Nick went for a stroll around the grounds. The peacocks on the lawn gave aristocratic cries, spread their colourful tails for the tourists to photograph, and strutted with a male vanity that Serena found singularly appealing.

'A wise investment of mine,' Nick drawled with satisfaction, looking up at the arched entrance of the manor with the twin crests blazing in the sun. 'One of my rare long-term purchases.'

Serena looked at him through her lashes. 'That's how you see me, too, isn't it, Nick?' Her voice was tinged with bitterness. 'A wise investment!'

He looked at her with a ruthless smile. 'You're part of the deal. You always were.'

She felt faintly sick, turning away, and thought, Why does he hurt me like this? Doesn't he realise how insulting he is? As though I'm a company he's been waiting to rearrange, turn around—instead of a woman with thoughts and feelings.

'Just think,' Nick drawled in those impeccable Bostonian tones, 'my children will inherit this and my first son will one day sit in the House of Lords!'

Angrily, she broke away from him. 'What children?' she snapped, green eyes flaring. 'There aren't going to be any children, because I'm not going to let you anywhere near me!'

His hand shot out to catch her wrist. 'Don't start that again!' he said tightly, staring at her. 'It was a casual remark, nothing more!'

'It sounded like ambition to me!' she said, hating him. 'But then you always were a ruthless, cold-blooded shark, and I'm not going to let you get your teeth into me, Nick Colterne! Not if—'

'I'm getting tired of your protests!' he bit out, holding her wrist with hard fingers. 'I thought we'd finally reached an understanding!'

'You thought you'd finally got me to agree to be a brood mare!' she spat, trembling.

'That's not all there is to it!' he said tightly. 'You know damned well I want to make love to you. Sure, I want an heir, too. But that doesn't mean I don't fancy you like hell.'

'But you wouldn't have married me if I hadn't been heiress to a title. Would you, Nick? You would just have tried to get me into bed, and if you'd failed, you would have shrugged and walked away.' Bitter tears stung her eyes. 'You don't want to make love to me. You want to make love to my title!'

Breaking away from him, she ran blindly across the lawns, scattering peacocks and tourists as she went, her heart hammering loudly in her breast as she reached the door of the private apartments and went in, slamming it behind her.

As she ran up the stairs she felt the hot tears stinging her eyes, and when she reached her bedroom they began to fall, her hands trembling as she put them to her face, drawing harsh gulps of air into her lungs, pain shooting through her heart like fire.

Nick was right behind her, slamming into her bedroom with demonic eyes. 'More arguments. More refusals. And for what? You know damned well I'll get you in the end, Serena. This is just a pointless waste of energy.'

'It's my energy,' she said tightly. 'I can do what I like with it.'

'Come to bed with me and I'll teach you a much better way to use it!'

'Get out!' she said in a clotted voice.

His mouth tightened. 'Don't order me out of your bedroom!'

'Why shouldn't I?'

'Because I've spent three years,' he said in a taut voice, 'driving myself round the bend to keep out of it!'

'With all your mistresses!' she said, eyes accusing.

'Mistresses or not—you couldn't have asked for a more patient husband!'

'Husband?' she spat contemptuously. 'A man who bought me for my title and my inheritance?'

'Yes, those are the facts, Serena. Are we going to run over them one more time, or shall we just take two paces backwards to that double bed behind you?'

'They're not facts!' she said, feeling the whirlpool of long-buried resentments building up to fever pitch inside her. 'They're home truths, Nick, and if you had any decency at all you'd be ashamed of yourself for what you're doing.'

He ran his hands through his black hair, drawling, 'I hate to say this, but I'm going to lose my famous patience with you if you don't stop this.'

'Go ahead!' she flung, tears slipping over her lashes. 'How do you think I feel? Do you have any idea what you've done to my life? I was twenty when I met you! My life was just beginning. I could have done any-thing—I could even have fallen in love with a man who might have loved me. But you didn't care about that, did you? You had to have me, didn't you? You had to try and force me to go to bed with you, and why? Out of lust! Lust, avarice, and greed!'

'All right, you little bitch!' he said in a slurred voice, and strode towards her, taking her shoulders in a vicious grip, ruthless intent in his hard face. 'It's home truths time, is it? Well, I think it's time I joined in, so let's get the rock-bottom truth out between us, shall we? Let's just—'

'You think you can win every argument, don't you, Nick?' she said shakily. 'But you can't win this one. I've finally told you exactly what I think of you and you know it.'

'Oh, have you?' he asked softly, blue eyes insolent. 'Want to take a bet on that?'

Hot colour flooded her face and she tried to jerk her gaze from his, but he caught her chin in a ruthless grip, his hard fingers hurting as he forced her to face him.

'What did you marry me for, Serena?' he bit out thickly. 'Come on. Let's have the truth on the table. The bed, I should say.'

'I wanted to save the estate and my parents from—'

'No,' he said tightly, unsmiling. 'Try again!'

'It's true!' she almost whimpered, barely able to meet his ruthless eyes. 'It was what I wanted and—'

'And what else did you want, Serena?' he asked

under his breath, and deliberately let his blue gaze move with searing insolence to her mouth, then her breasts, invoking shivers of searing desire. 'What else?'

'I didn't want that…!'

His teeth met. 'My God, how much longer do I have to wait to hear you say it?'

'To say what? What are you talking about?'

'I'll say it, then, shall I?' he said bitingly. 'Do you want it in gutter language or shall I stick to Latin?'

There was a tense silence. Serena stared at him, at his hard mouth and those ruthless eyes. He was right and they both knew it. But if she admitted it—she would be lost.

'You're beneath contempt,' she whispered, her pulses throbbing.

'I'm not beneath anything,' he said softly. 'I'll stoop to any trick where you're concerned.'

She stared hotly through her lashes. 'You're no gentleman…'

'But you're a lady, aren't you?' he said under his breath. 'So elegant and demure. Three years ago you stood at the window in that ladylike little dress, staring at me like the siren you are…' His eyes moved ruthlessly over her face. 'You can't hide it from me, Serena. I know exactly what you want.'

She did not fight as he pulled her arrogantly into his arms. Her heart was pounding too fast. Her hands were on his broad shoulders and she was staring at his hard mouth.

'Seductress,' he whispered mockingly, and bent his dark head, his mouth moving over her naked throat.

Serena's hands curled in his dark hair, her veins pulsing with excitement.

'Surrender,' Nick said thickly, his mouth wickedly exciting against her throat. 'Submit.'

She breathed faster, eyes partly closed. 'No...'

'I almost have you,' he whispered tauntingly. 'We're days from it, Serena. Tonight...tomorrow night...sooner than you think. And I'll savour every moment of it. I'll make you tell me, Serena, I'll make you say it out loud as I take you...'

The cruel mockery of his words were her salvation. She gained control of herself again, breaking away from him with angry determination, green fire in her eyes.

'No!' she said in a low, shaking voice. 'I'll never let you beat me, Nick.'

'You will, Serena,' he said softly. 'And you *will* tell me you want me.' He moved coolly to the door, a mocking, cynical smile on his hard mouth. 'But I'm not interested in forcing it. I can wait. I haven't been dying of frustration for three years. I'm not the one who's about to fall to their knees...you are.' He closed the door behind him and his laughter mocked her.

Serena stumbled to the bed, shaking from head to foot. The tension in her body was suddenly more than she could tolerate. It seemed to split her mind in two, one half refusing to listen to Nick's echoing words, the other straining at the leash, desperate to run to him in freedom like a whippet chained up for years in a dusty backyard.

Later, she dressed for the charity party. The green evening dress was quite stunning, a slim-fitting sheath that slid over her sensual curves in shimmering beaded radiance. Her long red-gold hair blazed like fire against it.

But her green eyes seemed to shimmer with emotion, with passion, with dark, brooding hunger, and she had to look away, her heart thudding, from the provocative young woman in the mirror who almost blazed with sexual frustration.

He was waiting for her in the living-room. He turned his dark head when she came out, and his face tightened as he caught his breath, a similar look of dark brooding hunger in his own eyes.

Serena felt sick with fear and excitement, saying jerkily, 'It starts at eight...'

His mouth hardened. 'Yes.' He strode to the door, wrenched it open, his eyes intent on her as she walked past him, electricity crackling between them as she brushed his broad shoulders accidentally.

A glittering array of cars was parked in the public car park—limousines, flashy sports cars and stately saloons. Caterers' vans littered the stable area by the café and a vast van in steel-grey was painted with the name of a popular jazz band.

A gorgon on the door demanded their charity tickets.

'No ticket, no entry,' she said, tight-lipped.

'I'm Nick Colterne,' Nick said with lazy charm, 'and this is my wife, Lady Serena Flaxton. I'm sure you won't refuse entry to—'

'Oh, good heavens!' stammered the gorgon. 'Mr

Colterne, forgive me! Your ladyship…oh, dear, how
stupid of me!'

They went in to find the cavernous Flaxton hallway
had been transformed into a vast banqueting area, very
Tudor, with charity organisers gliding about in Tudor
clothes. Serena noticed the women's costumes all had
the Boleyn hallmarks of long sleeves and French
hoods, and was impressed by the attention to detail:
Anne Boleyn had needed those sleeves to hide her
sixth finger, the hood a remnant of her days at the
French court.

Earl and Countess Archallagen were seated at the
top table, looking faintly bemused by the whole affair.
The other guests sat at the long table, drinking tank-
ards of ale in their smart twentieth-century dinner-
jackets, and the women glittered with diamonds.

'My daughter, Lady Serena,' the Earl introduced
them to the other people at their table, 'and her husband, Nick Colterne.'

Nick held Serena's chair for her, pushing it in coolly
as she sat down. He took his place beside her, one
strong arm flung out with proprietorial authority
against the back of her chair.

'Good evening,' he drawled coolly, studying the
other guests through his hooded eyelids, and the respect they showed him as they replied made Serena's
heart jump erratically.

'Haven't I seen you somewhere before?' Serena
asked the handsome young blond man opposite her.

'Possibly!' The young man smiled, looking elegant
and very debonair in his white dinner-jacket. 'I'm the
Viscount Hannon. But my friends call me Tony.' He

extended an aristocratic hand and shook hers, his blue eyes very young and admiring as he studied her.

Beside her, Serena noticed Nick was very tense, staring, holding his breath. 'My husband, Nick Colterne,' Serena said at once, gesturing to him.

'How do you do, old chap?' Tony's twinkling eyes moved to Nick and he extended his hand to him.

'How do you do?' Nick said in a hard voice, shaking hands with him.

'Tony's on the television, darling,' the Earl murmured.

'Oh, yes!' Serena smiled, remembering his face suddenly from the small screen. 'You have that late-night chat show, don't you?'

'Fame!' drawled Tony with a theatrical wave.

Serena laughed, amused by his self-mocking vanity. 'I must admit, I don't often watch your show. But I did see it the night you interviewed that comedian. Oh, what was his name…Australian man, very fat—?'

'Ed Alison?'

'That's it!' she laughed, green eyes dancing over his smooth young face. 'That was terribly funny. I was in tears laughing so much!'

'Hilarious!' Tony made a face. 'Why does everyone remember that show? I'll never live it down, will I?'

'He deliberately threw that bowl of custard over your head!' Serena said, and got the giggles suddenly at the memory of Tony, Viscount Hannon, going white with rage, not knowing whether or not to hit the man while the audience shrieked with laughter. 'I'm sorry!' Impulsively, she patted his hand. 'I shouldn't laugh, but it was so funny…'

Tony looked at her hand, then at her face. 'That's all right…' he said softly, the expression on his face suddenly changing.

Serena turned to Nick to explain and sucked in her breath at the look in his eyes. They were violent blue, rage leaping from them, and his mouth was a taut line.

'Darling,' Serena said shakily, 'Tony has a chat show and—'

'I heard,' Nick said with a bite of that cynical mouth, and looked at Tony with ruthless eyes. 'How did a young aristocrat get a job hosting a late-night chat show?'

Tony met Nick's hard, hostile gaze. 'Oh, you know,' he said with a frown, 'I just started at the bottom and worked my way up.'

'I doubt that,' Nick said curtly.

Serena flushed, annoyed by his unaccountable rudeness. 'Tony,' she said, patting his hand again, 'you must tell me all about life on TV. I'm sure it's very exciting.'

Nick leaned close and said thickly in her ear, 'If you don't stop touching his hand, I'll—'

'Please don't be a bore tonight,' Serena said, flicking him an angry look, 'or we'll have to start talking about your many mistresses!'

Nick went white, staring at her.

'I don't want to cause any trouble,' Tony murmured, frowning at them both.

'No trouble at all,' Nick said with a dangerous smile, and turned his attention to the very beautiful young actress sitting opposite him, a lazy, sardonic smile on his hard mouth as he flicked his gaze with deliberate sexual appraisal over her full breasts in the low-cut red gown and murmured, 'We were introduced, but I'm afraid I was too busy admiring your figure to remember your name...'

Serena caught her breath, green eyes flashing over the brunette with sudden violent jealousy. Nick was deliberately looking at her like that...with that sexual appraisal he normally reserved only for her...

'So what do you do, Serena?' Tony was saying in an effort to defuse the tension.

Serena stared at him, a red mist over her eyes, the jealousy and anger she felt over Nick's deliberate flirtation with the brunette too much for her to cope with suddenly.

'Serena?' Tony asked, leaning forward, frowning, a hand over hers.

'I'm an artist,' she said hoarsely. Then she struggled for dignity, and gave Tony a hot look through her lashes that she knew would have made Nick want to kiss her until her legs buckled. 'I've just had an exhibition commissioned...'

Dinner was a nightmare. Serena shot Tony flirtatious looks through her lashes, laughing while her stomach clawed with sick jealousy, and Nick continued to flirt with his brunette, not even noticing how she was looking at Tony.

Serena wanted to stick a knife in him. She found herself drinking too much, flirting outrageously, desperate to get Nick's attention, make him jealous, make him stop looking at that brunette...

After dinner a few celebrities made speeches. People

started writing out cheques. There was a lot of laughter and applause, then the band started to play.

The jazz clarinet echoed through the cavernous hall, and people began to dance in the space below the Minstrel's Gallery.

'Would you like to dance?' Tony asked her suddenly.

Serena caught the turn of Nick's dark head, heard his sharp intake of breath, and found herself defiantly rising to her feet with a bright smile, her green eyes glittering.

'Thank you!' she said, ignoring Nick's murderous blue eyes. 'I'd love to!'

Tony led her to the dance-floor. Serena's pulses raced with victory. That would teach Nick to flirt so blatantly, with such implicit sexual interest. How could he have done it…he must know it would be a knife in her heart?

'I love jazz!' Tony whirled her on the dance-floor, his young face lit with admiration as she swung, incandescent in the grip of primitive emotions, her red hair blazing and her sensual body supple in the green shimmering dress. 'And I absolutely adore you, Serena! Why haven't we ever met before?'

'I've been married for three years!' she teased lightly. 'That's why!'

'Madly in love?' Tony asked carefully.

Serena's eyes blazed with dark rage. 'No,' she said thickly, 'I hated my husband! I hate him…' She closed her eyes briefly, then looked up with horror, saying, 'Oh, God, I'm so sorry! I didn't mean that…I'm a little drunk…I shouldn't have—'

'Don't worry,' Tony said with a frown. 'We all get these moments…'

Serena gave a hoarse laugh, eyes wild with pain, sick pain stabbing into her.

'Are you all right?' Tony frowned.

'Yes, yes, I'm fine!' she said thickly, then produced a bright smile, ignoring her pain as she continued to dance. Nick was indifferent…the blood drummed through her, icy and sluggish: Nick was indifferent.

The music slowed. Serena looked back at the table. Nick was laughing at something the brunette had said, his cynical eyes inspecting her red mouth.

'Stay for a smoochy number!' Tony drawled, and pulled her into his arms.

In agony, she went, resting her bright head against his white dinner-jacket, dancing slowly. Closing her eyes, she tried to push the knife of jealousy out of her spiritual heart, but it was stuck fast, too deep, buried up to the hilt, and she knew then that the dark, ruthless stranger who was her husband would always strike the deadliest blow in any battle between them.

And she loved him for it; clinging to Tony's slim young shoulders, she drew a ragged breath, her body flooding with sudden, fierce love. He would always win. He was cleverer, deadlier, more ruthless than she.

Serena almost enjoyed the pain…

'Your hair's such a fantastic colour!' Tony was saying softly, running his fingers through it. 'Is it natural?'

'Yes,' she said, looking up, and over his shoulder saw Nick dancing with the brunette, his hard hands on her slender waist as she smiled and laughed and ran her hands through his thick black hair.

Serena went white, staring.

'What are you doing tomorrow?' Tony asked with a little frown. 'I'm in the area for a couple of days. We could get together. Maybe you could show me the estate?'

'Yes,' she said thickly, staring at Nick as the brunette kissed his hard cheek, left a stain of red lipstick on his tanned skin. 'That would be nice...'

Nick was facing her now as he danced, and his blue gaze seemed to meet hers with a sudden jolt, as though he'd known exactly where she was all along, and the look of ruthless mockery was more than she could bear.

'I'll call round at eleven,' Tony was saying. 'I know your family, of course, so I'll just turn up at the private apartments. Is that OK?'

'Yes,' she said vaguely, and felt her heart start to beat faster as Nick moved from the brunette, put a hand on Tony's shoulder, and pushed him coolly from Serena.

'My turn, I think,' he drawled with a lazy smile, taking Serena by the wrist and flicking her like a piece of silk so that she landed against his chest, her shaking hands on his shoulders. He started to move, his strong thighs intolerably exciting against hers.

Tony moved away but Serena hardly noticed, her eyes staring into Nick's hard face with a potent mixture of hatred and desire.

'You're playing a very dangerous game, my darling!' he murmured softly, and his voice was laced with implicit sexual threat.

'I'm not playing anything!' she said tautly.

'You're handling dynamite,' he said softly, his smile dangerous. 'Didn't you know that? And I'd hate to see you make a mistake. You'll get blown to bits if you do.' His strong hand moved softly, caressingly to her pale cheek. 'You won't like it if I lose my temper.'

'Go ahead and lose it!' she said fiercely, eyes blazing. 'I'm not going to stand around and watch you kiss that sexy brunette!'

'Certainly not when the charming young viscount is so obviously smitten,' he drawled, smiling lazily.

'Tony's very charming, yes!' she said thickly. 'And he hasn't looked at another woman since the dinner started, whereas *you* have lipstick on your cheek, and it isn't mine!'

The music stopped, forcing them to end their dance.

A muscle was jerking in Nick's cheek as he looked down at her. 'I'm warning you to stop this, Serena,' he said, his hands hard on her waist. 'Stop before it gets out of hand.'

Her mouth quivered with fear and excitement, but her jealous eyes saw only the red lipstick on his cheek and she said fiercely, 'Go back to your brunette! I want to finish my conversation with Tony!'

Turning on her heel, she walked angrily away from him, her green eyes blazing.

'No!' His hand shot out, caught her wrist, his voice a tense drawl, almost bored. 'Oh, no, Serena!' He drew her back, his smile savage. 'No, you damned well don't!'

'Let me go!' she said fiercely, trying to pull her wrist out of his biting grasp.

'No, Serena, I won't!' he bit out. 'This whole charade ends now! You're coming home with me!' He started to pull her off the dance-floor, his face a tense mask.

'For God's sake...' she began hoarsely, appalled at the scene he was making, people staring as he forced her off the dance-floor, his hand biting into her wrist as he strode, pulling her after him. 'People are staring! You're causing a scene!'

'I'm Nick Colterne, I'm your husband, I own you and this bloody manor and I can do what I damned well please!'

Serena stumbled after him, her face scarlet. Nick pushed through the little cluster of people at the entrance, shouldering through them, his face a taut, polite mask, and she had no option but to follow.

They were in the cool night air, the stars glittering in the sky, and Serena stumbled after him angrily as he strode, gravel crunching beneath his feet, towards the private Flaxton apartments.

When they reached the doors he pushed them open with the flat of his hand and dragged her in after him. He released her to close the door. Serena broke away from him, running breathlessly up the stairs to their suite.

Nick came after her at a terrifying pace.

'Leave me alone!' Serena shouted hoarsely, fumbling with the doors of the suite, running in, slamming the door behind her.

Nick came through, black rage in his eyes.

'No…!' she cried, backing, and then ran, her heart in her mouth, to the bedroom, going in and desperately trying to lock the door after her.

Nick kicked it open, a savage expression on his face. Serena backed, swallowing convulsively, her heart hammering as she stared at him, her green eyes huge in her white, appalled face.

'You went too far, Serena,' he said thickly. 'You went too far.'

Slowly, he began to loosen his tie.

CHAPTER EIGHT

SERENA stared, her hands clenching at her sides. 'You can't do this…'

'That was a very adult game you were playing,' Nick said with a dangerous smile, and his tie came off with a swish of silk, as he wrapped it around his fingers, then dropped it to the floor. 'If you're adult enough to use sex against me, you're adult enough to pay the price.'

She backed, her heart in her mouth. 'I didn't do anything…'

'You used sex against me, Serena,' he said softly. 'That's the one weapon you've always kept in reserve.' A smile touched his hard mouth, his blue eyes flicking over her body as he arched dark brows. 'Well…it's in play now, isn't it?'

'You're talking nonsense…' she whispered, backing, her legs suddenly coming in contact with the bed and stopping her where she was, her heart hammering as she faced him.

'Am I?' He reached her, stood in front of her, looking down at her through those carved lids. 'I doubt that, Serena, or you wouldn't be so damned terrified.'

'I'm not!' Her voice was ragged with it. 'I know I can stop you…'

'Sure,' he said softly, flicking his ruthless eyes to her breasts, and then raising a hand, deliberately sliding his strong fingers over her fiercely erect nipples. 'Well, well, well...sex really is in play, isn't it, Serena?' His blue gaze flicked up to hers. 'I've waited a long time to get it, my darling, and now—you're going to give it to me.'

She quivered visibly, staring at him hotly through her lashes.

'Shall I take you on the bed?' he asked coolly.

'I'll fight you!' she said through lips that seemed to pulsate with hot arousal.

He smiled, and lowered his gaze to her breasts. 'Take your clothes off,' he said softly.

She almost whimpered, breathing erratically, staring at him as though hypnotised, and that was the moment she realised she wanted this, wanted it so much that she had deliberately provoked it.

'No?' His dark brows rose. 'Then I'll have to do it, won't I?' His strong hands went to the zip of her dress, slowly tugging it down, and Serena shivered convulsively, heat flooding her veins, making her heart pound druggingly in her ears.

'Please don't,' she said hoarsely, denial struggling to rise feebly against overwhelming desire. 'Please... Nick...I'm sorry...'

'You flirted with that boy deliberately,' he said under his breath, stroking the shimmering dress down over her bare shoulders, his blue gaze on her breasts as they bounced free. 'You wanted to provoke me, and you did.' He smiled, stroking the dress down to her waist, leaving her bared. 'You always were a provoc-

ative little girl, and you've blossomed into an even
more provocative woman.'

Serena breathed thickly, staring at his hard mouth.
'I was jealous of you...you were looking at that brunette...dancing with her...'

'So you thought you'd even the score,' he drawled,
strong hands moving up to just below her breasts, not
touching them, watching her with a sardonic smile as
she shivered, her eyes hot and filled with unconscious
desire. 'Oh, yes...!' he said with a slow smile. 'You
keep looking at me like that, and we'll get along just
fine!'

'Don't go on!' she said in sudden appalled horror.
'Please, Nick...stop this...'

'Stop?' he laughed, his strong hands moving with
firm erotic power on to her full, hot, aching breasts.

'Oh, God...!' she whispered thickly, shaking, staring at him with green eyes that blazed dark hunger,
and he started to massage her breasts, watching her as
her lips parted and her eyes glazed, and a second later
his dark head was bending, his hot mouth closing over
her nipple.

Serena moaned a low, harsh moan of dark arousal,
and her hands went instinctively to his black hair,
thinking she would pull his head away, but she
didn't...she clutched it to her bare breast, shaking with
hot desire, her breath a ragged gasp.

Nick raised his dark head, inspecting her flushed
face with a ruthless look in his dark eyes.

Then he slowly pushed her until she fell on to the
bed, staring at him, shivering from head to foot, her
green eyes blazing with desire as he slid down.

He moved towards her on his hands and knees like a predatory animal, his dark head bent, and Serena's body curved with blatant sexual hunger, wanting him so badly that she was shaking with it.

He reached her, his mouth unsmiling, and slowly pushed her on to her back. As he slid one hard thigh over hers she felt the drumming blood pound in her ears, and as she met his dangerous eyes she felt the hair on the back of her neck stand on end with excitement.

His dark head bent slowly towards her. She could not look away. His hard mouth closed over hers in a masterful kiss and she moaned harshly, her mouth opening beneath his, her breath coming faster as her hands went helplessly to his strong neck and thrust into his dark hair.

The dark sexual landscape opened up to her like the hottest fires of hell and she was moving into it, her mouth open hungrily beneath his, her slender legs sliding against his as he kissed her with ruthless skill, demanding everything, his hard hands on her breasts as she started to breathe harder.

When those hard hands started to stroke her dress down over her hips she whimpered, heart pounding, and Nick just kept right on going, determined to have her, determined to drive her into the dark sea and smash her against the rocks.

The dress fell to the floor. He was looking down at her body, inspecting her nakedness as she lay there, blood throbbing violently, her eyes glazed with heat, and she wore nothing but a pair of silk panties that barely covered her. Nick slid his hand slowly to her

slim thighs and she gave a hoarse moan of ragged
desire that made his hard mouth curve in a ruthless
smile as his dark head came back to her, and his kiss
turned the heat up higher as his hand moved slowly,
slowly, higher…

'Yes…!' she breathed jerkily, twisting hotly beneath
him. 'Oh, God…Nick…'

He was unbuttoning his shirt, his face dark, watching her as he took the cuff-links out and threw them
to the floor. The shirt followed. He was back against
her, his hard hair-roughened chest electrifying as her
bare breasts rubbed against it.

His mouth burned down over hers. His strong fingers were sliding her silk panties down slowly, skilfully, over her slim hips.

Suddenly she knew this was the moment she must
stop him, but she couldn't, she couldn't fight the land-
slide of pent-up desire that was crushing her defences
in a torrent of hot pulses.

'Tell me you want me, Serena,' he said thickly,
ruthlessly, his eyes flicking with blackened desire to
her face. 'Tell me what you felt when you first saw
me. Tell me…'

She whimpered, closing her eyes, whispering
thickly, 'No…'

He laughed under his breath. 'Then I'll tell you,
shall I?' His hands continued to stroke her panties
down until he slid them off and they fell to the floor.
He was talking to her in that hard, ruthless way that
she loved, telling her everything that had run through
his mind, and as she moaned in rising excitement beneath him she felt his hard hands on her body and

knew she was approaching ecstasy, her blood drumming in her ears.

Nick was unzipping his trousers, pushing them down over his hips, and Serena started to pant, her mouth contorted in an agony of desire as he parted her slim, hot thighs with his, the hard throb of his manhood making her whimper as he slid between her thighs, his mouth on hers, and his eyes black with desire.

'Oh, Nick...' she said thickly, her hair standing on end with excitement. 'Oh, please...please!'

But he was merciless, and she started to sweat, her skin prickling with intolerable excitement, and then she felt the hard pressure of his manhood at her entrance and her breathing thickened, her heart banging harder as she felt him enter her, felt him thrust slowly, ruthlessly, until he filled her, and she choked out a fierce, guttural expellation of breath in ecstasy, her body now slippery with sweat as her heart banged that dangerous rhythm.

He was moving inside her, his face ruthless, and she was at fever pitch, staring at him through lids drenched with sweat, her blood throbbing faster, faster, faster... she thought he'd lose control, thought he'd waited so long for this that he'd go berserk, go completely out of control, go over the edge into ecstasy...and his heart was drumming even as he slammed into her, his face darkly flushed, his skin covered in sweat, his chest heaving and his limbs hair-roughened, slippery with hot perspiration, looking down at her with fierce dark eyes...and she wanted him to lose control...wanted it so badly that she was almost ready to claw at him...

But it wasn't him. It was her. It was her, panting feverishly as he ruthlessly took her over the edge and she felt the excitement spiral to explosion, taking her by surprise, forcing her up in gasping ecstasy against his hard body, her brain almost exploding as her eyes shut tight and her body went into hot, wet spasms, slamming against him with the scent of fresh sweat clinging to her skin, her hair, her eyes...out of control, moaning his name, and as the waves of violent pleasure dragged her into the whirlpool she knew she had always wanted this, wanted it from the minute she saw him, wanted it tonight as she'd flirted with that boy, wanted it forever...

Nick gripped her hips with iron fingers, slamming into her again and again with a face carved in barbaric determination until she finally subsided in a shivering wreck beneath him and watched him drive for his own satisfaction, his face hardening into a violent mask until he gave a ferocious snarl and jerked against her in his own release.

And what a release...his arms were shaking as he tried to support himself, his body flipping forwards, stationary for split-seconds as he cried out in a harsh, guttural voice then sucked in his breath, pulled back by an invisible thread and slammed against her again, his heart hammering as though he were dying.

Serena lay shivering like a pool of liquid heat beneath him, staring up at him, dazed. He collapsed suddenly, gasping for breath, his body as hot and slippery as hers, and their hearts drummed in violent unison as they lay together in exhausted silence.

They lay like that for a long time, breathing hard, and Serena felt her life had been changed by this experience. Emotions were flooding her, emotions she neither fought nor recognised. It was as though a floodgate had been opened and she was drowning in feeling.

Suddenly, Nick kissed her throat. 'Total surrender...'

She felt defenceless, hating him, loving him, unable to reply.

'That gives me absolute victory, Serena,' he whispered mockingly against her damp hair. 'Exquisite...well worth the wait.'

'You're so cruel,' she said hoarsely, and kissed his strong throat.

'You're right. I am cruel.' He laughed under his breath, his powerful body still a part of hers as they lay coupled. 'But it's been a long and bloody war. You made me fight hard, Serena. I enjoyed my victory. Every second of it.' He was taunting her. 'But most of all I enjoyed your pleasure...your frenzied excitement...'

She drew a shaky breath, running her hands along his damp spine.

'You relished your defeat.' He lifted his dark head, a cruel smile on his mouth. 'It was ecstasy for you...wasn't it, Serena?'

'Yes...!' she whispered, hating him.

'And it's not over yet.' The blue eyes grew more ruthless. 'You have an account to settle with me. It stretches back three years, and I have a long memory. Just think of yourself as a prisoner of war, my love. A captive aristocrat settling a debt with her conqueror.'

Serena whispered, 'If I'd given in on our wedding night…would you have been so cruel?'

'No,' he said with a slow smile. 'Not quite so cruel. But that only makes your repeated submission more exquisite for us both.'

'Why?' she asked, though she knew, and the excitement began to pulse in her veins as she heard his reply.

'I'll conquer you again and again,' he said softly, 'for the scratch you gave me on our wedding night…' he kissed her mouth, eyes mocking her '…for telling me you didn't want me in your bed…' he kissed her again, lingeringly '…for saying you couldn't stand the sight of me…'

'No…' she whispered, heart thudding in tortuous excitement.

His hands moved to her breasts. 'For saying you'd divorce me…'

She moaned, her nipples hardening under those strong, tormenting hands.

'You'd divorce me…' he whispered against her mouth, his manhood stirring potently inside her as he suddenly started to move against her, kissing her. 'Oh, would you, Serena? Would you, by God?'

His hard mouth closed over hers and she was delirious, her lips opening beneath his, a hoarse moan of pleasure coming from her throat as she felt his hard hands on her breasts and buttocks, his body moving forcibly between her thighs.

Her mouth was clinging passionately to his, her body like fire beneath him as he took exquisite revenge on her and she moaned out her surrender in a hoarse voice that shook with pleasure.

'You want me,' Nick was saying raggedly as he drove into her again and again. 'Say it...'

'Yes, yes,' she moaned as her body grew slippery with sweat again.

'Again,' he bit out thickly, his hands gripping her buttocks.

'I want you,' she gasped out hoarsely, her arms twining around his neck. 'Yes...yes...'

The room seemed to splinter into a thousand fragments of colour. Her heart was slamming violently. Suddenly she was flung into that dark ecstasy again, moving frenziedly against him, blinded by such exquisite release...such pleasure...such incredible pleasure...

A voice inside her cried, 'I love you.'

The pleasure went on and on. So did the voice. The words seemed to spin in her mind like light in catastrophic darkness, repeating again and again...I love you, I love you, I love you.

Then she was lying helpless and breathless, shaking uncontrollably as she stared up at him through damp lashes, her mouth slack.

As she watched him reach his own release she knew she was in love with him. His face was contorted with pleasure, his body shaking in those moments, and she felt moved by the sudden vulnerability she saw in the face she had hated for so long, her heart turning over with love as she listened to his fragmented cries of agony and ecstasy.

When he laid his damp head on her shoulder his body was shaking. Serena's trembling hands moved to stroke his dark hair. She was tentative, hesitant, unsure. Afraid to show him tenderness or love, though she felt it filling her like sunlight. And suddenly she understood poetry, love-songs, art…

She kissed his throat, her eyes tightly closed. I love you, she thought, and felt tears begin to sting. This was the root of her fear and hatred for three years…this powerful blaze of emotion that had suddenly landslided as he made love to her, breaking the barrier she had built three years ago to protect herself.

And she needed protection. Nick Colterne was the man she was in love with—but that didn't change him. It only changed her. Nick remained as ruthless as he had been before he'd met her, since he'd met her, and now that he had conquered her.

There was nothing she could do. She had fought her feelings for three years, and Nick's final victory over her was now complete. She was head over heels in love with him.

But he must never know. Never.

In the morning, Serena woke early. Dawn light filled the room.

It seemed her soul was new and her body was alive for the first time. Warm, sensual, beautiful…she turned with slow delight in her skin, red-gold hair falling softly over one eye to look towards her ruthless lover.

He was asleep, his strong face turned towards her,

one powerful arm flung around her as he slept on his lean stomach, long muscular legs splayed, one knee bent towards her.

Serena felt weak with love. Touching his face softly, she wondered how she had hidden her love from herself. It had been there all along, lying dormant, and she had been afraid to accept it because of the nature of the man she loved so deeply.

Suddenly, Nick's black lashes flickered on his hard cheekbones.

Serena's face was very close to his.

He opened his eyes slowly and met hers.

There was a heart-stopping silence, then he drawled in that lazy American accent, 'Good morning...'

She wanted to melt.

Nick studied her with a faint frown. 'What's going on inside that beautiful head?'

Serena lowered her lashes, hiding her love from him.

For a second he tensed, watching her. 'What are you thinking?' he asked under his breath, and then caught her chin, tilting her red-gold head back, his eyes narrowing on her sensual expression. 'About last night?'

Suddenly afraid, she said, 'Yes, I was thinking that I shouldn't have flirted so openly with Tony.'

His fingers tightened on her chin. There was a tense silence. Rage leapt in his blue eyes and she felt the warm sensuality disappear as anger emanated from his body.

'Don't ever mention another man's name in my bed again!' he bit out under his breath.

'You asked me what I was thinking,' she protested,

staring as his fingers tightened even further, bruising
her chin.

'Sure. And you just added to your account with me,
Lady Serena.' His voice bit out the title with harsh
sarcasm. 'Well, you may have enjoyed flirting with
that pretty blond viscount, but I'm the man in bed with
you.' His hand left her chin and moved down her naked throat invoking shivers as he slowly, skilfully
cupped her breast and stroked her nipple to erect obe-
dience. 'And I, Lady Serena,' he said thickly, 'am going to teach you another lesson in surrender. Understand me?'

'Yes...' she said breathlessly, and as his hard mouth
closed over hers their bodies were sliding together, silk
and steel, soft and hard, feminine and masculine.

Later, when her body was pulsing with blood and
sheened in sweat, she lay gasping beneath him, her
mouth against his damp throat, her hands shaking on
his powerful shoulders. She wanted to say, I love you.
She wanted to say it so badly, but she didn't dare,
couldn't risk his cynical laughter and the cruelty he
would show her. He had made it more than clear that
he was enjoying every second of his victory, and if he
knew she was in love with him he would use it against
her mercilessly.

Serena fell asleep in his arms.

When she awoke, Nick was gone.

Hurt, she looked at the clock. It was ten o'clock.
Why hadn't he woken her? She slipped out of bed,
nude, and suddenly heard the crunch of gravel under
wheels outside.

Running to the window, she looked out in time to

see Nick lowering the window of the Rolls-Royce limousine to speak to the brunette who had been at the party last night.

Pain shot through her. In disbelief she saw the brunette laugh, then the rear door of the limousine opening as she slid into it, looking very sexy in a short red summer dress.

As the limousine drove away Serena could not breathe, the stab of sick pain so deep that it was almost a real knife in her, making her whiten as she turned from the window, breathing erratically.

Last night had not changed Nick, then. He had married her for the reasons he had stated: lust and ambition, and no love would ever grow for her in his ruthless heart.

It was imperative she do something to stop the pain from growing. She took a hot shower, glad of the sting of water on her flesh and the rivulets on her face that hid her tears. Would this be the pattern of their marriage? That Nick would make love to her until she cried with pleasure, then leave her for other women when the fancy took him? It didn't bear thinking of.

When she emerged from her shower she blow-dried her hair, got dressed in an ivory silk shift dress and went downstairs to the living-room. Her face was set in white lines of pain.

'Hello, darling,' the Countess said with a vague smile. 'Your alarming husband left about half an hour ago. He told me to tell you he'd be gone all day.'

'All day!' Her eyes closed.

'Some telephone call,' said her mother, feeding a biscuit to a slavering dog at her feet. 'He was on the phone as soon as he came downstairs, and then he just disappeared.'

Serena winced. The brunette...

'Not to worry.' The Countess patted the hound and shooed it away. 'He'll be back tonight. Frightful party last night, wasn't it? I do hate these things...'

Serena left the room with a murmured excuse, and in the hall leant weakly against the wall. Nick Colterne had finally got exactly what he wanted. That she should love him for it was nothing more than self-destruction. Now he was starting to enrol a new mistress: the brunette he had met last night.

It hurt so much that she couldn't even cry. Just stood there, staring into a bleak future, her face white.

The doorbell rang.

Mottram came out of the kitchen with a cheery smile to answer it, passing Serena without noticing her agony, because Serena turned her head, averting her face from the girl, unable to let anyone see how tortured she was.

'I've come to see Lady Serena!' drawled a lazy, charming young voice. 'Is she around?'

Serena moved forward, relief filling her as she stepped behind Mottram and looked into Tony's charming, handsome face and his sparkling blue eyes filled with a warmth that she desperately needed.

'Tony!' she said, her voice hoarse.

'Serena!' He laughed, eyes racing over her, then made a face. 'Your handsome husband isn't around, is he? I'd hate to get my teeth kicked in. He looked absolutely murderous last night... dragging you off the dance-floor like that.'

Mottram's eyes bulged.

'Thank you, Mottram,' Serena said at once, watching her.

Mottram bobbed, disappointed at missing out on such juicy gossip, and slunk off into the hallway, her ears straining as she hovered a respectable distance away.

'My husband has gone out for the day,' Serena said in a low voice. 'He won't be back until later tonight.'

'Brilliant!' Tony said unashamedly, and caught her hand. 'So we can spend the day together?'

He looked young and carefree in jeans and an expensive white shirt from Simpson's. Handsome, too, in a blond 'English aristocrat' way. But he was not Nick Colterne, and he did not have that power, that masculinity, that ruthless mouth or that stark, irresistible sex appeal.

'I don't think it would be suitable, Tony,' she said with a sigh. 'I'm a married woman. People would see us...'

'But if your husband is out,' Tony said with a frown, 'and we only spend the day together—how can it hurt anyone?'

Serena's mouth compressed with a sigh. Looking into his eyes, she felt her pain show, briefly, and tried to hide it by flicking her lashes and staring over his shoulder while her mouth trembled.

'Serena?' Tony put a hand on her arm, concern in his face. 'My God, what on earth is wrong? You look absolutely devastated...'

'Nothing,' she said thickly, looking over her shoulder, aware that Mottram was lurking in the shadows,

taking in every word. 'Come on...' she walked out of
the door, closed it behind her and gave Tony a brief,
pained smile. 'Let's tour the manor. I'll tell you funny
stories as we go.'

It was a hellish day for her. All she could think of
was Nick, and she kept seeing him with that damned
brunette, kept remembering what he had said last night
about victory.

Their tour was quite diverting, though, and she told
Tony about various incidents in her youth when she
had lived in the manor with her parents, before Nick
Colterne had come along and blasted their lives into a
new and more dynamic existence.

At three, exhausted, they went to the stables and into
the café. Tony got her a cup of black coffee and himself a strawberry meringue cake, which Serena eyed
with vague amusement.

'You deserve to put on at least four pounds,' she
smiled, watching him lick his fingers as the last of the
meringue disappeared.

'I deserve a lot of things,' he said wryly. 'I don't
necessarily get them.'

Serena looked at him, catching the note in his voice,
and flushed.

'You used me last night, didn't you?' Tony watched
her with a frown. 'To make your husband jealous.'

Appalled, guilty, anxious to make amends, she
blurted out, 'Please forgive me, Tony. I was just so
upset and I wasn't thinking about what I was doing.'

'I understand,' he said with a vague shrug. 'It happens. I've done it myself.'

'Have you?' Her eyes drifted to meet his.

He smiled, blue eyes wry. 'Only when I'm in love with someone and want to make them jealous.'

She caught her breath, staring.

Tony raised blond brows, still smiling.

She flushed, saying huskily, 'Is it really so obvious?'

'Just a little around the edges,' he said gently. 'And he doesn't know. Does he?'

Serena wanted to put her head in her hands, but somehow she managed to just sit there, staring at a few granules of sugar on the oak table, and say, 'We've been married for three years. We weren't close until now. I didn't know I was in love with him.' Her voice grew shaky. 'But I know now.'

Tony watched her for a moment in silence. 'Is he in love with you?'

Bleakly, she shook her head.

There was another silence. Then Tony smiled, held out a hand and said, 'Let's go for a stroll around the grounds. 'I'll tell you about my own tragic love-affair...'

He talked quietly about a young actress he had fallen in love with, and the hell he had gone through, struggling not to let her guess how he felt.

'Then she died,' Tony said quietly. 'In a plane crash, last year.'

'I'm so sorry!' she said, squeezing his hand.

'I was like you,' he said, 'convinced she didn't love me. But after her death I was given her diary, and there it all was...page after page of it. How desperately in love with me she was, how hard she fought to hide it from me, too proud to let me know because I was...'

he laughed, raising blond brows '...too proud to let her know, either.'

The late-afternoon sun drenched them as they walked, hand in hand, and a peacock cry echoed across the lawns.

'I wish it were like that for me and Nick,' Serena said hoarsely. 'But it's not. It's very different.'

'It sounds identical to me.' Tony arched his blond brows.

'You don't understand,' she said huskily. 'My husband isn't like you. He isn't warm and loving and kind. He's—' She laughed incredulously, her throat dry as ashes. 'He's the most ruthless, cynical man I've ever met. I can't believe I've fallen in love with him. I must be out of my mind...'

Tony frowned. Cars were driving past, leaving the manor in droves. 'When is he coming back?' he asked suddenly. 'Before or after dinner?'

'After, I expect,' she said with sudden savage jealousy. 'He went off with that brunette this morning. I'm sure he'll be planning dinner followed by an expensive hotel bedroom...'

'Don't think like that,' he said with a sigh, then, 'Come on. I'll take you to dinner. You need to talk, and I'm a good listener.'

He took her to a quiet restaurant in the village. Flaxton had expanded to cope with the tourist trade which flooded in daily for the manor. There were now at least twelve restaurants and cafés in the town, and business was booming. Nick Colterne had revolutionised so many lives, not just hers. He was that kind of man. If only he were capable of love, too...

'What makes you think there's anything going on between your husband and Jasmine?' Tony asked as they ate by candle-light.

'Jasmine?' she said bitterly. 'Is that her name?'

'What makes you think there's anything going on?' he repeated lightly.

She lifted pained eyes. 'I saw him kiss her last night.'

'Trying to make you jealous?'

'I very much doubt it,' she said bitterly.

'But he's so obviously in love with you, Serena!' Tony stared at her. 'I didn't want to say it before because I didn't want to interfere. But I've never seen jealousy like that in my life. He was ready to tear me to pieces just for dancing with you!'

Her heart stopped, but she shook her head. 'He doesn't love me.'

'Then why the jealous scene?'

'He was furious because he thought I was making a play for you,' she said huskily. 'He thought I was—interested in you.'

'Well, what do you think jealousy is?' He laughed. 'Come on, Serena. The guy causes a jealous scene because you dance with another man, and you say, "But it wasn't because he was jealous!"'

Serena stared at him, hope in her eyes, then remembered Nick's cruelly exciting conquest of her, the things he had said...and the hope died like a fragile butterfly impaled on the needle of reality.

They drove home in Tony's white sports car. When he parked outside the Flaxton private apartments he turned to look at her in the dark interior of the car with a little smile.

'Know what to do now?' he asked, raising blond brows.

She laughed bitterly. 'Hang myself?'

'Come on, Serena.' Tony took her face in his hands, studying her. 'Don't turn your back on love out of hurt pride.'

'You're wrong, Tony. Nick doesn't love anyone, let alone me…' she whispered.

'Try it. Tell him you're in love with him.'

'He'd laugh in my face,' she said thickly.

'Defeatist,' he said, and kissed her mouth gently.

'Oh, Tony!' she whispered. 'What am I going to do?' Her arms went round him in a moment of camaraderie and fellow feeling, grateful for his kindness and advice.

Suddenly the car door was wrenched open and Nick's ashen face flashed before her eyes as he dragged Tony out of the car.

'Get out of there, you bastard!' Nick said savagely as he hauled the young man out with those powerful hands. 'I'll smash your face through the back of your head for this!'

'Steady on, Colterne!' Tony said hoarsely, hands up in self-defence.

Nick slammed him up against the car.

'No!' Serena scrambled out of the car, trembling violently as she ran full pelt round to where Nick stood, towering menacingly over Tony, his eyes vicious and his fist drawn back to deliver a punch.

'Tell him, Serena!' Tony shouted suddenly. 'Tell him!'

There was an agonising silence. Nick didn't throw the punch. He froze, staring down at Tony, who was defenceless as he stood against the car, his face white.

'Tell me what?' Nick said in a voice that sounded rusty.

Serena stared at the ground, her heart thudding a sick rhythm. She couldn't reply, too humiliated at the thought of what Nick would say if he knew she was in love with him.

Nick suddenly released Tony with a violent shove. 'Get in your car and go before I take you apart limb from limb,' he said in a low, shaking voice, but he didn't hit him, although his body was bristling with aggression.

Tony was white and shaken as he opened his car door.

Serena moved towards him. 'Tony, don't feel—'

'Get away from him!' Nick bit out hoarsely, and grabbed her by the wrist, his fingers like a vice, dragging her to his side, blue eyes glittering savagely in his white face.

'Do as he says, Serena,' Tony said, half in the car. 'But tell him. Tell him tonight, or it will get worse and—'

'Do you want me to break your bloody neck?' Nick swore hoarsely, taking an aggressive step towards him, bristling with violence.

'I'm going, I'm going.' Tony leapt behind the wheel and started the engine.

Nick held Serena bitingly by the wrist as they

watched the car reverse, turn, headlights blazing, and then drive away from the private apartments, red tail-lights flashing.

'What the hell was all that about?' Nick asked thickly, turning to her. 'What does he want you to tell me?'

She looked at him bitterly. 'Nothing. He was wrong anyway, so what does it matter?'

Nick's voice was thickly clotted with rage. 'What was he wrong about, or shall I guess? That I might give you a divorce if you genuinely fell in love with another man—is that it?'

Her green eyes shone with sudden tears. 'What difference does it make?' she whispered as a tear trickled down her cheek. 'Even if I told you the truth, you'd only laugh at me.'

'And what is the truth?' His hand tightened on her wrist. 'Are you in love, Serena?' His voice was splintering. 'You may as well tell me, you little bitch!' He seemed to suddenly lose control, hands moving to her shoulders, shaking her like a rag doll. 'Answer me! Answer me!'

He stopped shaking her suddenly, breathing hoarsely, staring down at her tear-stained face. Serena couldn't speak, just looked up at him in misery.

His hands left her shoulders. 'Go to him, then,' he said bitingly. 'I'll file for divorce first thing in the morning.'

He turned on his heel, striding into the Flaxton apartments and slamming the door.

CHAPTER NINE

SERENA stood there for a long time in the courtyard, just staring at the closed door. Divorce...? The very idea was intolerable to her. I'm in love with Nick, she thought in agony. How will I ever begin to survive a divorce from him? Suddenly she wanted to crumple where she stood and cry till her heart broke. But she had to be strong, because there was nowhere for her to go—nowhere but back into the apartments of Flaxton Manor where her hard, ruthless husband waited.

Slowly, she found herself walking into the apartments. They were dark and silent, like his heart, the man who would never love her, and who she loved to the point of insanity.

He was standing by the window, his back to her. Serena closed the door behind her, swallowing on a dry throat, her eyes running over him. He wore one of those impeccably cut black business suits, and she felt weak with love.

He turned as the door closed. 'What are you doing here?'

'I...' She lifted her red-gold head with fragile dignity. 'I have nowhere else to go, Nick.'

He gave a cynical smile. 'Don't tell me the viscount didn't invite you back to his place, because I don't believe it. I'm told you spent the whole day with him.' His voice was like the cold steel of a knife thrusting into her. 'He came for you this morning, just after I left.'

She watched him in silence, her face white.

'Around eleven, Mottram said.' His blue eyes were very hard. 'And it's now midnight. I assume he took you to bed, but didn't want to get mixed up in a divorce scandal. Very nasty. Certainly not the done thing. So he brought you back on the off chance that I wouldn't be here.'

'That's not what happened at—' she began tensely.

'Of course not,' he cut in cynically. 'It wouldn't be like that, would it? It would be…far more romantic than that!' He looked her up and down with those ruthless blue eyes. 'Well, my darling, it seems you've found your knight in shining armour, after all. It couldn't come at a better time. I've got what I wanted and I'm tired of the game. I certainly don't want any question hanging over the paternity of my sons.'

'I don't understand why you're saying this!' Her voice was hoarse, bitterly hurt. 'You must know Tony and I—'

'Wouldn't dream of committing adultery?' he cut in harshly. 'Of course not. But you'd get around to it sooner or later, and hell—why not? You're a sexy little piece. Even a fine upstanding aristocrat would want to—'

'Stop this!' she said fiercely. 'Stop it!'

He laughed at her protests, his mouth a hard cynical line as he looked her up and down with contemptuous mockery. Then his eyes met hers, and his smile faded.

Suddenly, he turned his back on her. There was a long, tense silence.

Then he said tightly, 'Regardless of whether you have or have not been to bed with him, I think we both know we've reached the end of the line.'

She was white, incapable of movement.

'We must be realistic,' he drawled. 'We were incompatible from the start. You didn't love me, and I didn't love you. For some time the arrangement has worked, but I don't see—'

'Nick...' Hot tears were suddenly spilling without warning over her lashes, trickling down her cheeks.

'It was just a sexual attraction, nothing more,' Nick cut in, his voice cynical. 'I kept you around because I hadn't got what I wanted from you. But I got it last night. As for the heir—there are plenty of penniless British peers with beautiful daughters. Makes no damned difference to me if—' He turned, saw her face, and stopped mid-sentence.

There was an agonised silence. Their eyes met. Tears were streaming down her white cheeks. She couldn't stop crying, but she lifted her chin with that fragile dignity, and drew a hoarse breath, trying to be brave.

'I quite understand,' she managed to say. 'A divorce...yes...'

Nick was very tense. 'Let me put it another way,' he said suddenly. 'If I gave you a divorce—would you marry him?'

She struggled to control her tears. 'Why on earth should I marry Tony?'

He gave a hard smile. 'You're in love with him.'

'No,' she said bleakly, shaking her head. 'I'm not in love with Tony.'

There was a pause.

'But you are in love...' Nick was very still.

Serena flushed. The silence dragged on.

His eyes seemed to burn on her face as he studied her across the room. Suddenly, he said very slowly, 'Did I ever tell you that I was in love?'

'No,' she said in agony, closing her eyes.

'Oh, yes,' he said. 'I've been in love for a long time now. I don't see her very often. But I haven't stopped loving her.'

'Really?' The jealousy, the pain, the unbelievable agony was crucifying her as she said in a fragile voice, 'Well, I don't...think...I want to hear about it now, Nick.'

'Why not, Serena?' he asked cruelly.

She gave a little moan of despair and turned her back on him, shaking hands covering her face as the last vestiges of her defences were obliterated by his cruel, casual words.

But his footsteps were coming towards her, his hands taking her upper arms and turning her to face him as his voice said deeply, 'It's you...I'm in love with you...'

Crying, she went into his arms. 'Don't torment me, Nick. Don't...'

'Serena,' he whispered against her hair, holding her very close.

'No...' Her voice was rough with tears. 'No more lies, Nick, no more pain...I fought for so long, but you beat me...you beat me hands down, and I love you…' She raised her head, mouth shaking, staring up into his face, whispering, 'I love you.'

He gave a hoarse groan, and then his mouth closed over hers with aching sweetness, the kiss so deep, so emotional that she clung to him, agony and ecstasy mingling as her arms twined around his strong neck and she wanted him to make love to her, even though she didn't believe him, didn't believe he loved her…

'I've loved you for so long,' Nick said thickly, dragging his mouth from hers as though he couldn't bear to, his lips remaining close to hers as he spoke, looking deep into her eyes. 'Since the moment I saw you, Serena. I was so sure you felt the same, so I just did what I always did when I wanted something badly: I took it. I thought once we had made love you'd tell me how you felt—and then I could tell you. But I couldn't risk it until then. And on our wedding night my whole strategy just fell to pieces.'

'But you were so hard and cynical.' She was staring in disbelief, afraid to believe him. 'You kept saying you only wanted my title…'

'I had to hide it,' he said deeply, holding her very close. 'I had to lie and pretend and hurt you. You were only twenty, and devastatingly beautiful. I was a very powerful man, head over heels in love with you. I was afraid you'd exercise that power over me. I couldn't let you do it. I had to take the whip hand. I had to convince you that I would never, ever love you. Otherwise, you'd guess.' He gave a rueful laugh. 'It was so obvious. If I'd taken the pressure off for one second you'd have put two and two together.'

Her eyes were stretched wide in acute emotion. She was beginning to believe him. It was incredible, but the ring of truth was in his voice and his eyes were so deep, so dark, so filled with love.

'When you refused me on our wedding night I knew I was in serious trouble. But I didn't know what to do. I stayed up all night, drinking whisky and staring out to sea.' He smiled grimly. 'I'll remember those damned palm trees forever! By dawn, I realised I was in a no-win situation.'

'I couldn't let you make love to me,' she whispered. 'Not on those terms. I would have felt used, abused—'

'I know,' he said deeply. 'I couldn't tell you I loved you—but you wouldn't let me near you unless I did. Stalemate.'

Serena closed her eyes with a sigh. 'Oh, God... we've wasted so much time.'

'Darling...' He kissed her lingeringly, his arms holding her very close. 'I wish this could have been ended then, but it wasn't. And one factor was your youth and inexperience. You'd gone straight from a little country boarding-school to a little country finishing school. Guarded by women, surrounded by girls, no contact with men or with life at all.'

'I was very innocent when I met you.'

'Too innocent to recognise your own feelings,' he said with a lazy smile. 'You fancied me like mad the minute you saw me—didn't you?'

Serena flushed and lowered her lashes, smiling shyly.

'I knew it,' he said thickly, holding her very close, kissing her head, stroking her hair. 'I didn't begin to get real confirmation of it until I came back to New York and got into bed with you...'

'That was very devious of you,' she said against his strong throat.

'Very,' he drawled, raising his dark head. 'Planned down to the last detail, I'm afraid. I'd been reading your schedules with a magnifying glass since we were married. I was waiting for a sign that you were ready for me.'

Her lashes flickered. She stared into his strong, handsome face and felt weak with love, her legs like jelly beneath her as she saw the extent of his love for her.

'My paintings...' she said in a voice filled with wonder.

'Yes.' He smiled, amusement in his blue eyes. 'You see, you'd never lived your own life, and I was strongly aware of that when I married you. After our disastrous honeymoon, I knew you'd find it difficult to find your feet. For months I read your schedules, expecting to find some sign of change. But they were always the same. One month in Hong Kong, two months in London, two months in New York, a month at Flaxton...'

'I just followed the crowd,' she agreed, nodding. 'I didn't know what else to do. I went to parties when I was invited, and mixed with your friends.'

'You weren't changing. If you didn't change— I couldn't break the stalemate.' He gave a harsh sigh. 'I knew there was no point in forcing it. If anything, it could have destroyed any hope I had of making you face your feelings for me.'

'Is that why you stayed away from me for three years?'

'Yes,' he said wryly. 'My God, I had to discipline

myself to do it. No contact from you except your
schedule, and how I pored over it, watching your every
move from a distance.'

'Nick,' she said, kissing his hard cheek, 'I would
never have guessed it. Never. You were always so
much in command. If anything, I thought you just
found me amusing. You used to toy with me, laugh at
me, mock me…and you could be so cruel. In the end,
I thought you really did hate me. You savaged me
sometimes…'

His mouth curved. 'I was getting desperate.
Especially this Christmas when we were here. I was
beginning to think your only hope of living your own
life was if I let you go. That was the worst point for
me. I seriously considered divorce, and it was hell,
Serena, because I was so deeply in love with you that
I thought I'd never be able to face life if I lost you.
But what right did I have to keep you in this awful
situation? What if I was wrong? What if you didn't
love me? What if I was just kidding myself?'

'Darling…'

'Then your schedule arrived and my heart missed a
beat when I saw it. You were moving. You were
changing. You were starting to live again and I saw
the light at the end of the tunnel as I finished reading
that schedule. I rang the bank and found out you were
withdrawing vast amounts of cash.' He laughed. 'I was
so excited that I nearly dropped everything and flew
to you. But then I thought—no. That's what you did
last time, Nick Colterne—don't you ever learn?'

'My darling,' she said softly. 'I love that in you.
You're so exciting…'

He kissed her and said, 'I gave you six months to

get back into life. When your six months were up I
came to get you. I chose New York because that had
obviously become the centre of your new life. It was
your strongest home territory. I knew you'd be at your
most vulnerable there.'

'Ruthless...' she said, adoring him. 'Quite ruthless.'

'I timed it so you'd be asleep. Even more vulnerable. I got into bed with you, took you in my arms,
started to kiss you—' He paused, then said huskily,
'And you whispered my name.'

Her heart stopped. She stared at him, lips parted.
Then she felt hot colour flood her face and said, 'I
didn't...did I?'

'Yes,' he said deeply. 'You whispered my name,
slid against me like a lover and kissed me very passionately indeed.'

'Why didn't you tell me?' she said on a gasp. 'I had
no idea I'd said your name...!'

He laughed and kissed her lingeringly. 'Darling, I
was playing the toughest poker game of my life. I
needed every ace I could get. You obviously weren't
aware of your feelings. You leapt out of bed, shaking
like a leaf, and demanded I go to the Plaza! That told
me your feelings were only just coming to the surface.
I had to hang around and fight it out until you surren-
dered.'

'I had no idea...' she said in wonder at his mind.
'Everything looks so different now. Everything.'

'Darling,' he said, kissing her, 'I love you. And I'm
dying to talk about all this in more intimate circumstances! Let's crack open the champagne and go to
bed...'

Serena went into the bedroom while Nick got a bottle of chilled Bollinger from the mini-fridge in the living-room. Happiness radiated from her; she felt light as air, undressing with quick grace. It seemed incredible that he loved her, a man like Nick Colterne...

When he came back she was in bed, her face flushed, radiant in a cream silk nightdress, watching with love and desire as he shed his black jacket, loosened his silk tie, began to unbutton that crisp white shirt.

'Nick...' she said with a sudden stab of sick jealous pain, her eyes flashing from his bare chest as he tore the shirt off. 'Your mistresses. I don't think I can bear to—'

'There are no mistresses,' he said flatly, and dropped his shirt, walking towards the bed, kneeling on it beside her, sliding his arms around her and kissing her red-gold head. 'I haven't even looked at another woman since I first saw you.'

'How can I believe that?' she demanded, her face suddenly pale. 'What about Monique?'

'Monique was always just a friend,' Nick reassured her. 'I'm surprised you didn't figure that out. Bony women have never been my type.'

'You kissed her in front of me,' she said, eyes darkening with jealousy.

'At the Plaza, you mean?' he smiled. 'I was hurt because you kept telling me to get lost. When Monique appeared out of nowhere I tried to make you jealous.'

'You went out with her that night,' she said. 'And stayed out until three in the morning!'

He laughed. 'No, Serena, I didn't. I went on a bar crawl to try and obliterate my despair. You'd just run out of the apartment, remember? I followed you down-stairs, but you'd jumped in a taxi, and I was too late.'

'I went to see some girlfriends.'

'I realise that now,' he said deeply. 'But at the time I thought you might have gone to see some other guy. You might have said my name in your sleep, but that's easily explained, darling. You were half asleep, after all. You could just have known unconsciously that it was me. It wasn't necessarily a sign that you were in love with me.'

'But you took Monique to the opera...' she pointed out, still wary.

'I needed her help,' he drawled with a rueful smile. 'To blow the Greyson set-up sky-high. It took me ages to explain to Monique that I needed to use her as a cover-mistress. She was very reluctant to ruin her rep-utation. She knew Greyson and hated him. In the end she agreed, on the proviso that I smash his head in if he did try and make a pass at you.'

'No...!'

'Monique likes you, Serena,' he said with a cool smile.

'I can't believe it...' she said. 'She was so convinc-ing as your mistress!'

'She's known me for years,' he said deeply. 'She knows I've been head over heels in love with you since day one. That's why she agreed to my little plan. But you can't imagine the agony I went through, lis-tening at that door.'

'That awful conversation I had with Phil...' She broke off with a gasp. 'Darling, you didn't hear any of my replies, did you?'

He tensed, staring. 'I assume you only considered

divorce,' he said thickly, 'because you hadn't realised how you felt, and—'

'No.' She touched his strong face with one hand. 'I did consider divorce—but I knew I couldn't do it, even then. I think that was the moment we really began to stand a chance together, Nick. You see, I told Phil I couldn't divorce you. Never.'

He stared, face grim. 'Is that the truth, Serena?'

'It's the absolute truth, darling,' she said softly. 'I can remember standing there, staring out at the Chrysler building, and knowing divorce was just not possible.'

'Why?' he demanded bluntly.

'Because I was in love with you, even then,' she said huskily. 'I found vast wellsprings of loyalty to you when Phil asked me to divorce you. I didn't know why and I hated myself for feeling such loyalty, but you can't fight your feelings, can you? I felt loyalty, baffling or otherwise, and that was that.'

He shuddered. 'Thank God you did. I would have stopped you if you'd been determined, but it would have been hellish. All I had was my belief that you'd fallen in love with me at first sight, just as I'd fallen for you.'

'Of course I did,' she said with wonder, studying his face. 'I can remember the day you arrived here, like a whirlwind of power and sex appeal...I absolutely flipped, Nick.'

'Say that again,' he drawled, a smile on his hard mouth.

'I flipped,' she said, looking at him seductively through her lashes. 'You were the sexiest thing I'd ever seen...'

'Oh, God...' he said thickly, laughing, and kissed her mouth.

Her hands curled in his dark hair. 'And it was so clever of you to bring me here, to Flaxton, where it all started.'

He tensed suddenly, lying very still. Then he slowly raised his head and looked at her with grim eyes. 'Yes, Flaxton Manor,' he said flatly. 'Your home and birthplace. And the last place in the world I expected you to meet the young blond viscount.'

Serena studied him, her lashes flickering. Then she said slowly, 'Why do you say it like that?'

His face grew hard. 'Because it was exactly what I'd been afraid of, all along. For the three years I played a waiting game, I knew a Viscount Hannon would one day come along. I knew what he'd look like, from his blond head to his aristocratic toes, and when he turned up out of the blue last night I was terrified. I tried to provoke your jealousy by showing Jasmine the kind of attention I'd always felt only for you.'

'You certainly provoked my jealousy—that's why I started to flirt with Tony.'

'And I was almost blind with panic. That's why I caused such a scene, dragged you back here and made love to you. The viscount had the right background, but I had the right mind and the right body. It was my ace—remember? And I felt I no longer had any option about playing it.'

'I'm glad you did,' she said softly.

'So am I,' he drawled, flicking her a lazy, wicked look. 'You can't begin to imagine how fantastic you were. I thought the back of my head was going to come off!' His strong fingers played lightly with her bare shoulders. 'It was everything I'd dreamed of since I first saw you.'

'But where did you go this morning?' she persisted, frowning. 'I saw Jasmine get into your car...'

'It was coincidence, darling. I had to go to London today. There was a business emergency that I simply couldn't avoid.' He drew back, studying her wryly. 'As my car drove away Jasmine came running over and asked me for a lift into town. I dropped her in the main street about ten minutes later. That's it. That's really all there was to it.'

Serena gave a hoarse laugh, shaking her head. 'And I went through hell all day because of it!'

'Is that why you went out with Tony?' he asked darkly, jealousy in his eyes as they blackened.

'Yes...and he spent the whole time trying to persuade me to tell you how I really felt.'

His hard mouth parted. 'You're kidding!'

'No,' she said with a faint smile, 'we talked about you all day and how much in love with you I was. Tony said I should tell you how I felt.' She outlined the sad story of Tony's late love.

Nick stared for a moment, then laughed wryly, drawling, 'Well, I'll be a son of a bitch! My greatest rival turns out to have been my strongest ally! I'm glad I didn't punch his face through the back of his head now. I only controlled myself because I knew you might be in love with him, and, if you were, I didn't have the right to stand in your way.'

'You hit Phil, though,' she pointed out.

'Yes,' Nick said with a ruthless flick of his brows. 'But he wasn't a threat—was he? He was a cheap little crook and nowhere near good enough to take you from me, Serena. I know my own worth, darling. And I certainly knew his: zero. Particularly after what he'd said to you about you divorcing me and taking me to the cleaners!'

He got off the bed suddenly, and went to get the bottle of champagne, ripping the gold foil with a cool, cynical smile on his face as he drawled, 'I'd like to take him to the cleaners, the little bastard!' He considered the prospect, his eyes narrowing.

Serena watched him through her gold lashes, adoring every powerful inch of him.

He looked up and caught the look in her eyes. 'Hmm,' he drawled softly. 'You like it when I'm ruthless, don't you?'

She felt herself curve like a cat, her shoulder close to her cheek as she almost purred, her lips parted, breathing unsteadily, watching him with her green eyes through her red-gold hair and wanting him to make love to her now...immediately...

Nick watched her through those carved lids, his eyes darkening. Slowly he put down the unopened bottle and walked towards her. He stood by the bed, unsmiling, then slowly reached out and flicked back the duvet.

'Nick...' she said thickly, sliding down into the bed, suddenly on fire as she curved her body in sensual provocation.

'What else do you like?' he asked softly, watching her.

'I love it,' she whispered, pulses thudding as she displayed herself to him, her body sensual in the silk nightgown, 'when you give me that look.'

'What look?' he said softly, and flicked his ruthless eyes to her breasts, making her nipples erect fiercely as she started to breathe faster, her body curving, watching him through her lashes with deliberate sexual provocation.

Slowly he slid into bed beside her, his hard mouth coming down over hers as she started to moan, felt his strong hands move over her, cupping her breasts, tugging down the lacy nightdress with skilled movements calculated to incite wild desire in her, and he started to whisper sweet words of desire, too, telling her how sexy she was, how much she turned him on, what had run through his mind when he first saw her, and then proving it to her, his face hard with ruthless power as he stripped her, stripped himself, and slid between her quivering thighs to take her. The ecstasy was unbearable; she was helpless against him as he gave her the kind of lovemaking she had wanted from him for so long...

Later, when she was a quivering wreck of hot flesh beneath him and his damp head was laid on her shoulder, his ragged breathing and fiercely drumming heartbeat told her he felt as much for her as she did for him.

'Darling,' Nick murmured against her cheek, 'has it occurred to you that you might already be pregnant?'

Serena held him very close, whispering, 'I hope I am. It will make everything even more wonderful.'

He kissed her lingeringly. 'I think we should call our first son Robert, after your ancestor.'

'That's a nice idea,' she said, smiling up at him. 'What made you think of it?'

His hard mouth curved in a smile. 'I've thought it

since I first met you. You inherited his red hair and his sex appeal and his incredible luck. It strikes me as no coincidence that you were born just when the Flaxton family needed another stroke of luck.'

She laughed, intrigued by the idea. 'That never occurred to me.'

'You're not American,' he drawled. 'You don't have romantic notions about history and particularly about quirks of historical destiny. But I do, and I remember how completely right everything felt when I first drove up to this house...when I first saw those Tudor turrets. I felt as though I could hear trumpets playing, and when I got out of the car I stared up at the house and saw you. I completely lost my breath as our eyes met. Just lost it. Punched out of me.'

'And nothing was ever the same again...' she said huskily.

'Nothing,' he agreed, eyes darkening, and as he lowered his dark head to kiss her she heard those trumpets play too, and felt the future unfurl in the sunlight like a bright, glorious banner of love.

Harlequin Romance®

Delightful
Affectionate
Romantic
Emotional

Tender
Original

Daring
Riveting
Enchanting
Adventurous
Moving

Harlequin Romance—the
series that has it all!

HROM-G

Harlequin® Historical

From rugged lawmen and
valiant knights to defiant heiresses
and spirited frontierswomen,
Harlequin Historicals will
capture your imagination with
their dramatic scope, passion
and adventure.

Harlequin Historicals…
they're too good to miss!